GIDEON AND THE MUMMY PROFESSOR

Books by
K A T H L E E N   K A R R

It Ain't Always Easy
Oh, Those Harper Girls!
Gideon and the Mummy Professor

GIDEON

AND THE

MUMMY PROFESSOR

KATHLEEN KARR

FARRAR STRAUS GIROUX
NEW YORK

For Renée Cho

GIDEON AND THE MUMMY PROFESSOR

ONE

"Ladies and gentlemen! Enter with me now into a world of vast darknesses, glittering heat, mysteries beyond our ken ..."

Gideon yawned. Another night, another town, another stage. This was a very small stage in a very small opera house with an equally small audience. Gideon stood manfully in the wings by the crank that operated the panorama roll looming over him. The moth-eaten curtain had been pulled aside, revealing his father, the one and only "Mummy Professor," launching into his pitch.

"Cast your eyes behind me to the unique, the original Panorama of the Nile! A work of art completed after much study and by many hands to be the marvel of the nineteenth century! Note the Sphinx himself sitting in splendor before the greatest of the pyramids. What ancient genius carved this Wonder of the World? What ancient mysteries decreed its erection—" His voice broke off and lowered to a fierce whisper. "The Sphinx, Gideon!"

Gideon jumped, and cranked for his life. Thank heavens, there came the Sphinx, unwinding from the far roll of the movable backdrop fifteen feet across the stage. The boy sharpened up and concentrated on the formidable professor—who hated to be called "Father"—dressed in black tails with fraying satin collar, white waistcoat, and a softly knotted white tie. Around his head was wrapped a turban of maroon silk, deftly arranged so that the edges of his dark, silver-streaked hair could still be seen, emphasizing the noble features and ascetic look of his handsome face. Gideon's outfit was a smaller-scale match, except for his headdress, which was gold. The professor claimed it shone nicely in the flickering stage lights, and gave a touch of fantasy to the proceedings.

George, the third member of their traveling troupe, received no such splendid sartorial trappings. He lay there now, on a table in the center of the stage, covered only with a homespun bedspread liberated from a recent boardinghouse. They'd had to pawn his embroidered coverlet to pay their fares on the last steamboat. If things didn't improve before they made it to New Orleans, the panorama would be the next to go. They daren't pawn George. Not after . . .

Gideon caught his father's hand signal and cranked

another few yards of painted scenery out of its bolt. Now all three of the great pyramids were spread out for the audience's edification.

They'd picked up the panorama in London, in their balmier days on the return trip from Cairo, where his father, then known merely as Stephen K. Tompkins, Esq., had spent a number of years as an underling to the U.S. consul. Egypt was where they'd picked up George. It had been a mere whim of his father's at the time. A joke about an extra traveling companion, someone to lighten the tedious hours of the journey with them. Sometimes it seemed to Gideon that everything had been downhill since.

"Now we are voyaging up the Nile. Yes, *up,* my friends, though the compass points south. Past the step pyramid of Saqqara, past the most ancient capital of Memphis. Sail with me on a single-masted felucca, with exotically handsome Nubians tending to the rudder . . ."

Gideon was working up a sweat. The professor was moving to Thebes and the Valley of the Kings exceptionally fast tonight. He'd skipped the whole piece about Antony and Cleopatra, and hadn't even paused for his usual discussion of the mastabas, the oldest of the pharaohs' tombs.

The professor must be hungry, or, more likely, thirsty. He'd claimed the inn they were stopping at brewed an uncommonly fine ale. That had to be the single uncommon thing about the place, aside from the size of its Mississippi cockroaches. Gideon despised cockroaches. Give him an honest desert scorpion any day.

5

". . . and Edfu, the temple of Horus, the falcon god . . ."

Galloping dromedaries! Gideon laid into the crank again. At this rate, in a minute they'd be at Aswan, then the last of the ancient temples at Abu Simbel. And they were. There was polite applause from the scattered crowd, before Gideon was introduced as the professor's assistant, a rare albino pygmy from the regions south of the Atlas Mountains. Gideon winced. He always hated that part. Granted, his stature was small for a fellow almost thirteen, and he was white-blond, like his long-since-departed dear mother. But his hair was lank, not tightly curled, like that of pygmies he'd read about. And his eyes were a rather fine blue, actually, matching those in the miniature of his mother, the mother he couldn't even remember. One of these days he'd put on a growth spurt, just to spite his father.

Gideon trotted forth and made his bow, and his father continued.

"And now, ladies and gentlemen. The moment you've been waiting for. The moment you've come for. Beneath this shroud lies a mystery stranger than any you've seen thus far: the remains of a genuine pharaoh of ancient Egypt. And before your very eyes we shall unwrap him. For the first time. The only time since his burial eons ago." The professor grasped one end of the bedspread. Gideon grasped the other. The audience leaned forward in their seats, expectant. The pause was milked until, on practiced cue, the cloth was finally whipped away.

"I give you Ramses Amenhotep Kom Ombo III!"

6

George looked sicklier than ever this evening, Gideon thought. He didn't take well to this nightly ritual. At the moment only his eyes were revealed, surrounded by the folds of tobacco-colored linens that encircled his mummified corpse. The linens had, in fact, been stained in tobacco juice in an effort to give them the proper patina of age. George's original wrappings had worn out back in St. Louis. Now it was those very eyes—or eye sockets, at least—that glared balefully at Gideon. "Sorry, George," he whispered, as he always did.

"Get on with it, Gideon!" commanded his father, *sotto voce.*

Gideon began stripping off the linens as his father elevated the mummy. Soon George was revealed down to his navel. They never went any farther than that out of respect for the finer sensibilities of the ladies who might be in the audience.

Gideon stepped back and waited for the *aahs* from the audience to subside. As usual, folks were straining their necks, and as usual, the professor played upon this curiosity and made his challenge.

"There might be some among you unwilling to believe in the authenticity of Ramses Amenhotep Kom Ombo III. Do not leave the theater in that state of mind, my friends. Instead, walk up here and inspect this wonder of the ages for yourselves . . ."

A few folks began moving from their seats before the professor added the clincher: ". . . unless, of course, you choose to believe in *the curse.*"

One or two people sat down quickly, while a large,

belligerent-looking fellow shouted out, "Hogwash! The perfessor's just hiding a fraud!"

"Come up, then, by all means, my friend," the professor invited. "Surely the pharaoh will not hurt one with a scientific interest. How could he? He is but a shell of his former self. His stomach, his lungs, all his organs have been removed long since."

"Let's hear the curse, then!" shouted another from his seat, as the burly man paused with indecision in the aisle.

The professor raised one hand as if in blessing, gazed up to the heavens—or at least the ceiling of the opera house—and dramatically proclaimed: *"Let the hand raised against me be withered! Let them be destroyed who attack my name, my foundation, my effigies, the images like unto me!"*

The professor had made that one up some time back, in Cincinnati, possibly. He liked the way it sounded vague and threatening at the same time. The hulking farmer, still standing, didn't seem particularly impressed, however. Finally decided, he let out a bellow of a laugh and came on. His heavy boots shook the steps leading up to the stage. Then he stood in front of George in his patched pants, smelling strongly of livestock.

"He don't look too healthy, at that." Two thick fingers were raised to touch the mummy, and before the professor could fend them off, those fingers were poked right into George's stomach.

"Please, sir! Have consideration for the remains of the dead!"

8

The fingers were removed, but poor George was the worse for it. He always had been a little crumbly at best. The bewildered farmer stood staring for a moment at his fingers covered in gray, four-thousand-year-old mummy dust. His eyes met Gideon's, and the boy was startled by the revelation that shone from them. Belief in George? In the curse?

The farmer's attention returned to his hand as he took two blind steps backward, stumbled, and plummeted off the edge of the stage. He landed with a resounding thud and remained sprawled on the floor, stunned and still. An instant of silence followed before pandemonium broke loose. The audience let out one communal scream of panic and bolted for the door.

The professor glanced at his son. "Perhaps we should make our departure with all possible dispatch, Gideon."

"Yes, sir."

Gideon ran to let down the stage curtain, while his father packed the panorama. Then there was George to deal with. Letting his bandages lie loose, Gideon began wrapping him as quickly as he could in the bedspread. As he turned to pull the cloth around the mummy's leathery back, clasping him gingerly to his own chest, there was the clink of something hitting the floorboards of the stage. Blindly, Gideon bent, reached for the object, and stuffed it in his trousers pocket. Then he finished his wrapping job and bore George to the rear stage door.

〜

At that very moment, a mere thirty miles upriver, another scene of agitation was unfolding. Emmanuel Wistover—late of Cairo, London, and New York— soldier of fortune, embezzler, and cad extraordinaire, was pacing the confines of his shabby rented room, berating his fate and his companion.

"Shall we never catch up with Tompkins and his young cur? I've been tracking them across this wretched country for months, always a few steps behind. And you, Naseem"—he turned on the woman—"always a few steps behind me. If you hadn't lingered in that shop today, we never would have missed the steamboat. I could have had my hands on Tompkins—and his mummy—this very night!"

Naseem, swathed in vividly colored silks, her fine, coal-black hair half-hidden in a knot beneath a head-cloth, nodded submissively, brushing invisible specks from the shoulder of Wistover's smoking jacket.

"Will you cease and desist, woman!" He shrugged away from her attentions. "Why I ever saddled myself with an Abyssinian slave evades me at the moment. Price, most probably. You did seem a bargain at the time. Male valets these days do expect to be paid regularly. Still, I should have left you cowering at that camel market in Aswan, along with the donkeys and sheep. Who knows? A pasha might have favored you for his harem." He caught the flash of revulsion that flitted across her face. Wistover chortled. "No, even with your Cleopatra-like features, that was highly unlikely. There are too few pashas left in Egypt these days. More likely you'd be herding goats for a Bedouin tribe at this very moment, instead of traversing the world under my tutelage." His pace turned momentarily into a strut. "Keep my generosities in mind, Naseem, else I might forget your one saving grace, the fact that you are incapable of answering me back."

Naseem lowered her almond-shaped eyes. She was, indeed, mute, but there were moments when those dark orbs could have spoken volumes. She raised a dusky hand as if to tug at Wistover's sleeve, to remonstrate with him, but was shrugged off again.

"Enough!" He was examining himself in a mirror now, admiring the lavish waves of his thick chestnut hair, the straight line of his thin, pointed nose, the well-shaven triangle of the chin that completed his long face. All was satisfactory, as usual. "Hand me my embroidered waistcoat and the playing cards; then you may be excused to your own quarters. It's time I strode forth to wrest some remuneration from the local citizens. If we're to be stranded in this backwash of civilization till the next boat arrives, someone will have to pay the board."

Safely back in their room, Gideon carefully rewound George's linens before tucking him upright behind the door, out of harm's way. Next he checked the buckles on the tarpaulin covering the panorama roll lying on the floor. Their hasty departure might have caused his father to be less careful than usual. It wouldn't do for the paintings to be injured before they made it to New Orleans and the engagement there that might return them to solvency. The professor, of course, always left these little details to his son. The saloon downstairs had already summoned him.

Finally satisfied, Gideon began stripping off his costume. He'd best try to catch a nap on the lumpy bed before his father's return. Gideon was a light sleeper, and drunken snores were not conducive to his rest. Removing the trousers first, he held them upright to straighten the seams. As he shook them, something fell out of a pocket and rolled into the corner next to George.

"What in the world . . ." Gideon muttered to himself before retrieving the object. It was not large, but heavy in his hand, and cool. Gideon moved to the candle by the bed. The thing in his hand caught the flame and glinted back at him, almost shimmering, a cold, green light encrusted in golden sparks.

Gideon stared, then collapsed onto the edge of the bed to stare some more. Finally he looked over to George, whose eye sockets glowered through the shadows.

"The accident tonight! You've been holding back on us, my friend. What do you suppose the professor will make of this?"

Sober in the next morning's light, his father sat on the rumpled bed, still in his nightshirt, inspecting Gideon's find.

"May my eyes not be deceiving me! A scarab, the

ancient Egyptian symbol of rebirth!" He held it out to catch a few rays from the sun streaming in the window. "See how finely the insect has been carved and etched in the stone—there's the figure of Serket, one of the goddesses who protects the dead, with her arms around the central cartouche, and the sun of everlasting life shining above her—"

"What do the hieroglyphs inside the cartouche say, Professor?" Gideon stood before him, fully dressed, as he had been since dawn, waiting for his father to awake. "And those worked into the gold on the scarab's base?"

His father squinted more closely and hedged. "Well, a magnifying glass might be useful for this close work. But only consider, Gideon! A larger emerald than I would have thought possible!" He gazed in awe, mouth agape.

"Are you sure it's not just glass, Professor?"

The look turned scathing. "The Egyptians wouldn't bury a pharaoh with mere glass, Gideon. Nor would they set mere glass within prongs and a base of fine gold, as this has been. Only the best and finest materials would be saved up for eternity."

"But we don't know that George was a pharaoh. That's just something you made up for the show, like George's name, and the curse. He could've been anybody, a slave—"

"None but the very wealthy could afford the mummification process. That sets our mummy well above the common crowd. He had to be a royal retainer, at the least." The professor struggled to pull his attention away from the glittering gem. "Why are you fighting this good fortune, Gideon?"

Gideon swallowed. There was no point in arguing further when his father got into this frame of mind. "Then the gold must be worth something, too, sir. Will it solve our problems?"

The professor's eyes were still glazed over—with shock, or maybe hunger.

"Perhaps, Gideon. Perhaps."

A rough knock rattled their door. Gideon and the professor both started guiltily. The scarab danced in the professor's hand. Gideon plucked it up and shoved it back into his trousers pocket.

The knock came again, even sharper this time.

"Yes, what is it?" The professor used his stage voice, smooth and commanding.

"It's me, Cleary, the landlord. I ain't got nothin' agin you, Professor, since you already paid me up, fair and square. But Jed Smithers, what got clonked by your mummy's curse last night?"

The professor had pulled on his trousers and already had the door open. "Yes?"

"Well, he's come to, roaring like a lunatic. He and his three brothers is on their way over, fightin' mad, and fixin' to tar and feather you and the corpse both."

"The brothers. Are they all as big as this Smithers?"

"Heck, no. Jed, he's the runt of the litter!"

Gideon had started tossing their belongings into their

satchel as soon as he'd pocketed George's treasure. Now he handed his father his shirt as the nightgown was thrown at him. In another moment, the professor had pulled on his boots and toppings in sight of their host.

"Thank you, my good man. A loyal innkeeper is a rare and wondrous thing." He flipped a coin from his vest pocket at Cleary before settling his watch fob into place and adjusting his traveling jacket.

Gideon was getting worried. "I can hear a ruckus out the window, Professor. Maybe you could dispense with fussing over the lay of your collar, just this once—"

His father frowned at him, then directed himself back to Cleary. "If you'd kindly show us to the back door . . ." He stopped and searched for another, larger coin. "And if you'd look after my panorama until I call for it? I assure you, you'll be richly rewarded."

"What about George?" Gideon asked.

"He will join us. I suspect we haven't plumbed the depths of his mysteries as yet."

Gideon staunchly shouldered George, picked up the valise, and staggered down the rickety back stairs in pursuit of his father and their host.

About two miles south of town, while scrabbling through the brambles and briers on the Mississippi's edge, Gideon got very tired. He set down the satchel, calling to his father up ahead, who'd finally taken his turn carrying George.

"Professor?"

"What is it, Gideon?" George lurched off a shoulder and fell, snagged on the same brambles.

"Have we gotten far enough away from Eulah Landing and the mob yet?"

As they'd slipped behind the main street of the town, Gideon couldn't help but notice, between the gaps of frame buildings, that Jed Smithers had apparently rounded up more than his brothers. Every able-bodied man in the environs appeared to be rampaging down the dirt road toward the hotel. From the quick glances Gideon had snatched, they seemed to be in a celebratory mood, all right. He had no intention of being one of the guests of honor at their revels, though. The three of them had been booed and hissed before, but he didn't care for the sound of this tar-and-feathering business.

"Well . . ." The professor swiped at the thick, dark locks of hair that curled damply around his sweating face. His nose, almost Roman in proportions, twitched slightly. From fear?

"Don't you think, Professor, maybe we ought to put some consideration into what we do next? Besides run? I mean, we seem to be in somewhat of a more difficult position than this time yesterday. We've got George, but without the panorama, we haven't got an act. Also, I noticed that in your desire to impress the landlord back there you seem to have given him just about every last cent we owned."

"The scarab, my boy. Don't forget the scarab."

Gideon's belly rumbled. "Pretty as it is, I can't see that bauble filling our stomachs."

"Sold to the right party, it will feed us for any length of time, Gideon. Keep that in mind." The professor stopped abruptly. "You do still have it? You haven't lost it in our precipitous flight?"

Gideon felt for the lump in his pocket. "I put it on the side without any holes."

His father's sigh of relief was heartfelt. "Perhaps we'd better consider a more appropriate hiding place."

"Back inside George?"

The professor gave the mummy a considered glance. "No. I'm not quite sure I trust George to that extent."

"Really, Fa—I mean, Professor—don't you think maybe you're taking your own stories a little too far?"

"Gideon!"

"Yes, sir."

"If you're rested, perhaps we should proceed. New Orleans is a fair walk downriver if you take into account the fact that we haven't even reached the Louisiana border yet. If we sell the emerald scarab for what I hope, Cleary may wallpaper his scrofulous inn with the panorama, for all I care. We'll have enough funds to embark first-class for Europe and a life of ease."

Emmanuel Wistover, trailed by Naseem, stepped off a boat onto the levee of Eulah Landing, where the professor and his entourage should still be performing, according to the roughly printed broadsheet that Wistover had torn from a wall thirty miles upriver. Wistover was feeling pleased with himself. He'd managed to book passage on a transient steamboat, a full day ahead of the scheduled packet. Success was within his grasp. He strode over to one of the locals lounging against a bale of cotton. A big, brawny, country fellow he was, all cowlicks and untrimmed beard, smoking a clay pipe.

Wistover patted his perfectly pomaded hair. "Excuse me, my good man. Would you be kind enough to point in the direction of a decent hostelry?"

"Iffen you mean a hotel, there ain't but one in this town."

"Ah." The search was narrowing. Wistover smiled. Then his anticipation got the better of him. "You wouldn't happen to know if an itinerant performer known as the Mummy Professor might be residing there?"

The small eyes on the yokel's large face squinted suspiciously. "Might you be a friend of his?"

"A friend?" Wistover blithely ignored the danger signals. "My dear man, the professor and I go back a long way, a long way indeed. Why, his very mummy was discovered in my presence. You could say we were almost like brothers—" Wistover stopped as he found himself suddenly in the viselike grip of the stranger.

"Willy Joe!" the man bellowed. "Round up Jed and the rest of the boys. Fast! And get the fire going under that tar pot again. We got us a first-rate replacement for the perfessor!"

Dusk found Gideon, the professor, and George farther down the Mississippi. They'd passed one small settlement in their travels, but had circled it in the fear that their reputation might have preceded them. They had just settled on a sandy spit below a willow-covered bluff, next to the river itself. George's head was pillowed on a stone, his legs out flat, pointing toward the Mississippi. He had an air of relief at having survived the day, Gideon noted while pulling off his boots and rubbing at his sore feet.

"Mummies aren't anywhere near as light as they ought to be, Professor. I don't see how we can keep carrying him like we are. Not without some food."

"Tomorrow, Gideon. I promise that tomorrow we'll stop in a town to find food and work things out."

"Tomorrow isn't soon enough. I'm hungry now." Gideon was so hungry that he'd thought of nothing else for the past several hours. He'd missed his supper last night and had had no breakfast today, or any other meal, for that matter. He watched as the professor pulled a hoarded cheroot from his coat pocket. It was followed by a match. The match was held up, ready to strike against a boot sole.

"Stop!"

His father halted in mid-act. "What is it now, Gideon? Can't a man indulge in a little relaxation after a strenuous day? I need this cigar."

"How many more matches have you got?"

"I don't know!" The professor's voice was petulant.

"Count them. Please."

His father turned out his pockets with ill grace. As Gideon had suspected, there was only the one match.

"We're going to need that to start a fire; then you can light your cigar. Unless you were planning on snuggling up to George for warmth tonight."

"I wasn't planning on anything—"

"You never do, Professor. You never do."

"I don't care for that tone of voice, young man. I am still your father, your only living relation. Until such time as you are capable of caring for yourself . . ."

But Gideon had already wandered off down the beach to search for driftwood.

Gideon was fishing by the first light of dawn. He'd never fished in his life. It was desperation that did it. He'd fashioned a hook from the lady's hatpin that held George's wrappings together, connected it to the string that kept the mummy's feet from bouncing apart, and tied it all up to a sapling branch he'd found while hunting for firewood. For bait, Gideon dug several worms out of the embankment behind them. Now he sat by the Mississippi, trolling his line, praying for a miracle.

The professor was still asleep by the fire Gideon had kept banked all through the long hours of darkness. It was amazing how chilly it could get at night this far south. And it was only September. Gideon shivered, and hunched farther within his jacket. There was no way the three of them could survive walking all the way to New Orleans. They hadn't the experience or the stamina. George's wrappings were getting more tattered by the mile. As for his father, he was soft, always taking the easy way out. That should put him in a quandary now, as there didn't seem to be any simple way to walk downriver to New Orleans. But the professor hadn't worked that out yet, and wasn't likely to, still sleeping.

Gideon flicked his line. He supposed his father needed him. The professor always needed someone. It was family connections of Gideon's mother that had gotten Stephen Tompkins the posting in Cairo. But now she was long gone, and her parents, too. And his father hadn't managed to hang on to his position. He should have known better, tried harder. Life was easy for a white man in Egypt.

Gideon felt a tug on his line and jiggled it expectantly. Nothing. He let it stray out again. Egypt was all he'd known until the age of eleven. He thought about the walled compound they'd lived in, the servants that had tended to their every need, the excursions to the pyramids and up the Nile as his father dabbled in Egyptology in his many spare hours. Maybe it was because he'd ignored the job that he'd lost it. But then there was also that quarrel with the strange man Wistover. And the last eighteen months, wandering half the world, most of it in a native land Gideon had not remembered, and was still uncomfortable with.

Another tug came, stronger this time. Gideon pulled his line, full of hope. Maybe the scarab was a good sign. All of them could use a little resurrection about now.

Emmanuel Wistover lay flat on his stomach atop the packed dirt floor of an abandoned log cabin on the edge of Eulah Landing. Naseem hovered over him, still plucking sticky feathers from his hair and rubbing turpentine over the skin that hadn't been protected by his clothing. Wistover was seething.

"Tompkins shall pay for this. He shall pay for every moment of my ignominious suffering. I swear he shall!"

Above him, unseen, Naseem's lips curled into a rare smile of satisfaction. She ripped a scale of tar a bit too roughly from Wistover's outstretched wrist. He yelped.

It had been a small fish, but a fish nevertheless. It gave Gideon and his father enough strength to struggle up the bluff, thread through cane fields, and find the next settlement. There was a steamboat waiting at the landing, loading cotton. The professor had had enough. He bartered his last possession of value aside from the scarab—the prized pocket watch and fob that had been a wedding gift from Gideon's mother—for passage and board to New Orleans.

Gideon was not sorry to stand by the railing and watch the boat pull away from the Mississippi shoreline as the boilers slowly built up steam. His fingers fondled the scarab in his pocket like a talisman. He turned to speak to his father, but the professor had already left for their cabin. He was probably attending to his neglected shaving. The professor believed in presenting the best personal image possible.

In a few days, just a few days, their troubles could be over.

TWO

The Mississippi had widened to a greater breadth than Gideon had ever seen on the Nile, except when it was in flood. From the top deck, he took in the bustle of the port of New Orleans with satisfaction. There was a jumble of ships moored three-deep; clustered passengers; loaders and hawkers. There were extravagant flowers and wonderful smells. With a few gallabiya-clad natives and minarets, it could be almost as colorful as Cairo. It was good to be disembarking upon land and civilization once more.

It was also good that they had a little walking money. The professor had used the two-day trip aboard the steamship to their advantage. He had, in fact, been working almost constantly the entire time, and not on archaeological lectures. Truth be told, Gideon's father was a creditable hand at polite games playing. He'd once mentioned to Gideon that it was one of the few accomplishments he'd acquired from his Harvard education—aside from entrée to his wife's blue-blooded family. But the professor hadn't been playing whist and bridge aboard the *Lulabelle*. He'd had to lower his standards to American poker. Gideon didn't mind, so long as his father won.

Gideon himself had passed his time prowling about the boat, watching the Negro stokers fuel the hungry maw of the furnace, the deckhands load cotton at their frequent riverside stops until the *Lulabelle*'s lower deck was so close to the river it was almost taking on water. He engaged in polite conversation with the pilot, learning a little about the charts that guided the boat around the curves and sandbanks of the treacherous river. But mostly he stared, mesmerized, at the huge paddle wheels revolving at the sides of the ship.

All of it was a welcome change from dingy opera houses and the exhaustion of their escape. He and the professor had both been so busy that they hadn't had time to give George a thorough examination. Gideon had broached the question to his father during the first and only meal they'd managed to share together in the ship's dining room. It was between the soup and the meat course, as vast tureens of mashed potatoes and platters of roast beef had begun to circulate around the long table.

"About George, Professor?"

"I'd like that rare slice in the middle, Gideon. What about George?"

Gideon speared the choicest portion and slid it onto his father's plate before helping himself to a lesser offering. "Now that we have a little time to recollect in tranquillity, as Mr. Wordsworth put it—"

"*You* might have the time and tranquillity, Gideon. I, however, have another appointment at the tables directly after dinner is dispensed with. Do stop hovering over the gravy and pass it along."

"Are you suggesting that I delve into the depths of George's mysteries on my own?"

The gravy boat froze in the professor's hands. He glanced pointedly at the messmates closely surrounding them, lustily gorging, and lowered his voice. "Greed at table is but a sign of grasping cupidity. Observe where you are. This is neither the time nor place for this conversation, Gideon. And you are to undertake *nothing* without my presence. Is that understood? Nothing. Sleeping . . . *mysteries* should lie until we find ourselves in a more appropriate environment."

Gideon had complied with more relief than regret. Yet he couldn't help speculating. Was the mummy hiding more treasure? On the one hand, Gideon was anxious to learn the answer to that question. On the other, passing George's haunted, vacant stare in the tight confines of their cabin, Gideon had the feeling that maybe a dissection was something he'd rather not perform. It would come to that, of course. They'd have to destroy George to learn what other secrets he might possess. Gideon shivered. The professor could be procrastinating for similar reasons, not just because he distrusted a ship full of potential rogues. George deserved something better than this final violation. What he truly deserved was to be returned to Egypt for a burial on the west bank of the Nile, in the sands of his homeland.

A brisk clap on the back startled Gideon.

"Ready to take on the world, my boy?"

Gideon glanced up into his father's face, flushed with its recent successes, then down to the dangling watch fob obviously just retrieved out of hock from the captain. "Yes, sir. I think I might be."

This time they could afford a carriage to take them to a hotel. And the professor didn't choose any broken-down stopping place, either.

"Image, my boy, image," he responded to the question on his son's face as they entered an establishment obviously well above their means. "We must have the correct surroundings in which to conduct our negotiations."

"Aren't you afraid of the theater people finding us? The ones we're supposed to put on the show for?"

"The show will proceed, Gideon. A gentleman completes his contractual obligations."

"But we skipped Natchez—"

"*Harumph.* An occasional lapse in the greater interests of economy is sometimes unavoidable. The passage was good straight through to New Orleans."

Gideon tried to digest his father's reasoning. "And the panorama? Are you planning on giving the show with just George? And is that really why we haven't finished exploring him? So we'd have part of the show still intact?"

"Hush." His father peered around the ornate lobby they'd just entered, and made believe he was counting their pitiful pile of possessions once more. "Ears everywhere, you know. As for the panorama, a trifle. I've left the *Lulabelle*'s captain with directives to procure and transport our property from Eulah Landing to New Orleans on his next run. The panorama will arrive here in good time for the opening of our engagement in two weeks. With that guaranteed, it occurred to me that George's ultimate demise could be postponed. Let him go out in a blaze of glory, as it were, after the final admiration of the good people of this fair city. And now"—the professor was guiding Gideon toward the hotel's polished mahogany reception desk—"and now perhaps we'd best acquire suitable accommodations."

Suitable accommodations turned out to be a two-room suite overlooking the bustle of the Vieux Carré. The geranium-festooned balconies beyond the French windows of the sitting room and bedroom looked down at the Cabildo and Jackson Square beyond. The spire of St. Louis Cathedral blocked out some of the view, but still, it couldn't be considered shabby.

27

George had been transported upstairs by one of the hotel's servants. The man had been a little careless in tossing the bundled mummy onto the floor of the sitting room. Coincidentally, perhaps, he'd mashed his fingers in the room's heavy door on his way out. Gideon stuck his head out the same door to follow the servant's soft curses down the hallway as he nursed the hand. He finally closed the door and turned to George appraisingly.

"Feeling a bit sprightly today, old boy?"

"What's that, Gideon?"

"Nothing Professor. Just muttering to myself." But Gideon proceeded to prop George against a chair by the window, surprised to find himself taking pains to unwrap the mummy's head down to his neck. He was overcome with the strangest sensation that now that he'd received his reprieve, George wanted to watch the view, too.

"We've got to get to New Orleans." Wistover was pacing again, this time in a lodging in Natchez. "Tompkins never showed for his engagement here. It could mean he's still running scared ..." He stopped to scratch at a pinkish, raw strip of skin on his cheek. "On the other hand, it is possible that he may have found something." He waited for a response from Naseem, then remembered for the thousandth time that it would never be forthcoming. She just lingered in the background, looking disconcertingly smug. No matter. He'd always found his own conversation irresistible.

"Yes. We'll book passage immediately. New Orleans is the end of the line. Where could he go from there?" Wistover halted before the bureau mirror. His hair had been destroyed by those medieval louts. It would take months before the bare patches from the tar were filled in again and his beloved locks restored. He'd have to purchase a becoming hat. And a pistol. This business with his old rival had now gone beyond conversation.

The professor placed announcements in the New Orleans papers. He didn't refer to the scarab, or even the emerald, for that matter. Just noted that a rare ancient treasure was being made available for bids by discriminating collectors. As for the treasure itself, they'd decided that perhaps the safest place for it was with Gideon, after all. Who would suspect an undergrown boy of harboring such a thing? They purchased a leather amulet bag, of which there were many being sold in the markets of the city by old Negro women, and secreted the thing around Gideon's neck, under his shirt. When the operation was completed, Gideon heaved a sigh of relief. The scarab had been wearing the lining of his pants pocket disconcertingly thin.

Wistover sat in a modest hotel room in the American Quarter of New Orleans, paging through the selection of newspapers he'd purchased upon arriving in the city.

"There must be something about Tompkins's theatrical engagement. In all the bigger cities he always publishes an overblown account of his lectures. 'Thebes, Babylon, and Nineveh,' something on that order. With a lot of nonsense about cuneiform and hieroglyphics thrown in. What little he understands of hieroglyphics wouldn't get him past the first line of one of my papyrus scrolls. And he calls me a scoundrel! Bah!" He threw down the first set of sheets and picked up the next.

Naseem carefully retrieved her master's rejects, folding the pages smooth, surreptitiously reading the commercial and personal notices on the front page. Her eyes lit up in interest at one spot. She glanced at Wistover, thought to herself, then shrugged slightly and glided over to his chair.

"Yes, what is it? Can't you see I'm busy?"

Naseem pointed to the tightly worded notice above her finger, one eyebrow raised in question.

" 'Rare ancient treasure,' " Wistover read aloud. "Naseem, you are truly a gem. A paragon among personal servants! Perhaps my pains over your literacy— those long days at sea teaching you the English alphabet—were not in vain. They've found something! It has to be them! 'Viewing by appointment, after eight of the evening.' " He rose. "Prepare my best suit. And oil the pistol. I shall dine early, then pay a visit to the 'Mummy Professor.' "

The sitting room of the suite had been readied for the occasion. George had been moved out of harm's way to the bedroom. The other obvious differences included the well-stocked bar on the sideboard and the swathe of midnight-black velvet that draped the oval marble-topped table now set strategically in the center of the room, under the oil-lamp chandelier. A ring of candles in glowing silver sticks edged the table and threw further light upon the object resting on a small pillow of black satin.

Gideon admired the scarab, picking it up to give it another spit-polish with the cloth in his hand. The goddess Serket seemed to wink at him, then tighten her grip around the central cartouche. Gideon grinned, touched the beetle's minuscule head for luck, and returned the jewel to its bed, making sure it was placed to catch all the sparks of light cast around it.

The professor was putting the final knot into his maroon turban. "Not bad, eh, my boy?"

"It's almost a shame to have to sell it, sir."

"Don't go soft on me now, Gideon. If you'd seen the looks the hotel's manager has been giving me—"

"We have been here almost a week, Professor, and they haven't seen the color of our money yet."

"Nor are they likely to if we don't find a buyer quickly. And eating all our meals in the hotel dining room is getting tedious. I'd much rather be tasting the other myriad epicurean delights of this splendid city."

"You can't put them on the tab."

"Precisely. My *Lulabelle* earnings are gone. And I can't very well be gambling on the hotel's premises. Doesn't fit the image." He smoothed down the silver-streaked hair around his temples. "For that matter, I'm not quite up to chancing the cards outside the hotel yet, either. From my brief forays of observation into the local wagering dens, it appears that the gentlemen of New Orleans have exceptionally low boiling points."

Gideon flicked a speck of dust from the velvet covering. "So it's all or nothing tonight. Care to share with me who we're expecting?"

Ignoring Gideon's tone, the professor consulted a slip of paper. "One Jonathan Dupree, of the city; Marcus Weatherbee, no given address; and a Claude Christmas."

"Christmas?"

"Unusual, isn't it? I consulted with some gentlemen in the saloon. Seems it's an old New Orleans name. His mother was some sort of legend years back."

"Not Annie Christmas?" Gideon had been spending his spare time around the docks, and that name had come up more than once, in a swearing capacity.

"Something I should know about?"

"Only that she was a flatboat woman, stronger than any ten men. And a fair hand at business, from what I gathered."

The professor slipped his hand into his jacket pocket to feel the small gun he'd purchased with the last of their funds. "I think I stand prepared, Gideon."

Gideon shook his head. Even at the shop it had seemed a very inadequate-looking weapon. "I hope so. I'd hate to see us gulled, or worse, at this point."

"You have a suspicious mind, Gideon, and I don't think it came from my side of the family."

"Are you suggesting that my sweet mother—"

"I know your mother was and is an angel, Gideon. All too well. Her parents, however—"

There was a timid knock at the door. Gideon quickly covered the jewel with another scrap of velvet. He adjusted his own turban, then went to answer the summons.

A short, portly, middle-aged gentleman entered, calling card in hand. "Jonathan Dupree. I have come to the correct room?" His glance flickered from Gideon to the professor to the candlelit table. "Ah, yes. It appears that I have, indeed."

"Welcome, Mr. Dupree." The professor nodded toward the sideboard. "Would you care for a small libation? Sherry, perhaps, or bourbon?"

"Bourbon. Neat."

Gideon scampered to prepare the refreshment. He had consulted his father about the local drinking habits, and even had on hand bowls of fresh mint, sugar, and expensive but rapidly melting ice, should a mint julep be required. With his back to the men, Gideon popped a fragment of the precious ice into his mouth. No point in having it all wasted, and the room did seem to be warming up. He turned with the drink as another, more peremptory knock sounded at the door. Gideon swallowed the ice, coughing.

"Your drink, sir. I'll tend to the door."

Their next guest had to be Claude Christmas. He was bigger than Jed Smithers back in Eulah Landing. He was also dressed more fashionably than Jed would ever be, if a little loud. Shaggy brown hair fell to the shoulders of his fitted maroon frock coat, from which a pink satin waistcoat blossomed forth. Gideon didn't know what to think of Christmas's roughly square, scarred face, and he surely didn't care for the thick bulge of the gun grip he saw protruding from one side of his waistband, either. Then again, practically all the men in New Orleans carried guns. He'd seen them on the streets, but hadn't gotten accustomed to them as yet—not even to his father's.

"Bourbon, Mr. Christmas, sir?"

Christmas acknowledged his introduction with a grin that softened his well-traveled face. His eyes flitted over the room. "See you've got the fixin's of a julep there, son. Whyn't I mix it up myself? Proportions got to be just so."

"Certainly, sir."

Gideon hovered by the sideboard, watching the ritual. Strangely, he thought maybe he could like this man. His slow, soft drawl was so different from his appearance.

"Powdered sugar be better, son," Christmas commented as he stirred the glass and added extra ice. "It gentles a strong bourbon."

"I'll keep that in mind the next time."

"You do that."

A third knock sounded on the door as Christmas raised his glass to his lips. Everyone in the room stiffened expectantly. Gideon broke the tableau first, moving toward the door and reaching for the knob.

"This would be our final guest, Mr. Weatherbee—" He froze as the door opened. It wasn't.

His father responded with more aplomb. "Ah, Emmanuel. I was wondering when we'd have the pleasure of your company again. It has been such a long time. Do join us."

Emmanuel Wistover strode in, pistol in hand, primed and pointed.

Gideon gulped. "A little sherry, Mr. Weatherbee— er, Wistover?"

"Not unless you can find me a third hand." Wistover motioned them all with his gun to the center of the room, around the table. "Let us dispense with the usual niceties. I believe it is time that the viewing of the treasure begin. Do the honors, please, Stephen. You always did have a flair for the dramatic."

"You've never been a slouch in that department yourself, Emmanuel." The professor's hand fluttered around the scrap of cloth. "What happened to your hair? I do hope you haven't been ill."

Wistover's answer was spit out with quiet fury. "A small altercation upriver in Eulah Landing. It seems I was mistaken for a friend of yours."

Gideon caught the glimmer of satisfaction on his father's face, and the confusion on those of the other two men. Dupree coughed delicately. "If you two gentlemen would prefer to discuss your business privately, I'd be happy to view the treasure at another time." He began a mincing step away from the table.

"On the contrary, sir." Wistover waved the gun in Dupree's direction. "I would much prefer that you stayed."

"Of course, of course." Dupree scampered back. Christmas said nothing, just took another big gulp of his julep.

"The treasure, Tompkins." Wistover's slight smile was sardonic. "Remember?"

"How easy it is for the mind to forget under the weight of circumstance." The professor cleared his throat and began his set speech without even a tremor. Gideon was impressed. Professionalism told.

"Gentlemen. I am about to unveil for your edification and enjoyment an object the likes of which you have never seen. The likes of which no one has seen—save my assistant and me upon its discovery, of course—in lo, these thousands of years. It is an object which I can guarantee as being of an antiquity reaching back in time to the land of the pharaohs, to the Eighteenth Dynasty." His hand hovered.

"Do it, Tompkins. Or shall I?"

"That won't be necessary, Wistover." The professor's long, well-cared-for finger and thumb grasped the edge of the covering cloth. "Gentlemen. The treasure of Ramses Amenhotep Kom Ombo III!"

The cloth was lifted, and the scarab glowed up at them. It seemed bigger than ever, bigger than life. Even Gideon was startled by the unearthly beauty of it. All stared, mesmerized.

Then Wistover collected himself and broke the spell. His free hand snatched out to grab the treasure, and he bolted for the door. Christmas woke next, pulling his own gun from his belt. There was an exchange of shots, and Wistover, apparently unscathed, gave up on the door to dart for the bedroom. Gideon, closest, ran after him first.

Inside the dark room, Wistover's shape was skirting the beds and making for the balcony. They were but on the second floor. The villain could easily swing over the side and disappear into the streets below. Gideon made ready to leap at Wistover, to wrestle him to the floor, to thwart him in any manner possible. It became unnecessary. A shape by the window, unmoving, yet somehow looming larger, interfered with the escape. With an oath, Wistover tripped, lost his balance, and fell headfirst over the low wrought iron of the balcony itself.

As Wistover's scream filled the air, Gideon heard a small, solid clunk on the floor of the balcony. He ran over and pocketed the scarab as the professor and his other guests entered the bedroom, candles in hand. They rushed for the balcony, hanging over it to peer below, shouting.

"Police! Police!"

"Hold the thieving villain!"

In the newly lit room, Gideon ignored the growing street sounds of a gathering crowd and the din his father and Dupree were making. Instead, he turned to the mummy and solicitously propped the dislodged figure upright once more.

"So, George," he whispered. "Is it possible you don't care much for Emmanuel Wistover, either?"

The men were turning back from the balcony.

"To think that scoundrel got off with the scarab!" The professor was beside himself.

"And those people in the street just dusted his jacket and helped him limp off!" Dupree was shaking his head sorrowfully.

Christmas said nothing, but he was staring hard at Gideon. And that was small wonder, for Gideon was grinning like the proverbial cat.

"What is it, boy?"

Gideon calmly walked back into the sitting room, his elders following, and deposited the scarab on its bed. "Mr. Wistover was in such a hurry to depart that he left something behind. We're still in business, Professor. Would you care to start the bidding?"

The professor held up his hands with a smile. "As my assistant suggests ..."

Dupree reached out to touch the stone, then drew back as if scorched. "No." His voice was mournful. "No, I must regretfully decline, tempting as it is. The stone has an aura of ill luck about it." He gave the scarab one final, wistful look, then backed toward the door. "Gentlemen . . ." And with a nod, he was gone.

The professor turned to Christmas. "Perhaps you feel the same, sir?"

Christmas barked out a short laugh. "Hardly. My interest has been merely piqued by the little performance you arranged this evening. My congratulations to you, Professor."

"Sir, if you think I would arrange such a thing!" The professor had arranged many another performance during his career, but here he stood innocently accused. "On my honor—"

" 'Honor' is an easy word, particularly in this city, Professor Tompkins. I am, however, amused by your little trinket." He reached out a large hand and stroked it. "My mama always had a soft spot for such pretties. It'd be an emerald, wouldn't it? Nice faceting, too. How many carats you reckon it is?"

The professor swallowed. "Close to a hundred, I'd say."

"Would you consent to having it weighed by a jeweler, Professor?"

"Certainly. But its value, as you can see, goes far beyond its mere weight as a precious stone—"

"My eyes are as good as yours, sir." Christmas stroked the scarab again. "Whyn't I just leave you with a little down payment, as a show of good faith. A sort of holding price."

"Returnable, sir?"

"Half to keep—for your trouble—and half to return, if I change my mind." Christmas pulled a wad of bills from a money belt and shuffled through them until he was satisfied. "Here you go. You meet me Monday next at Devol's on Canal Street. Eleven of the morning. If I'm not satisfied, we'll part amicable like. If I am, we can bargain."

Gideon watched his father try to hold back his enthusiasm as he accepted the notes. Dixies they were, a whole pile of ten-dollar bills. And half of them to keep. Gideon's own palms began to itch. Not for the cash, but for thinking how to keep the professor from spending it all outright before next Monday. Three days was a long time to sit on ready money. Then Christmas was gone. Gideon locked the door and turned to his father.

"How much?"

He was still counting the bills, a third time. "Five hundred. Take off your turban, my boy, we're going out on the town!"

"What about the hotel?"

"I shall leave them with a down payment to our account. Come Monday, we'll book a ship out—"

"And our engagement?"

"—departing directly after our theatrical engagement, of course. We'll explore George a little more in depth at that time, too, as we'd already planned. There would be no point whatsoever in losing a ready mark like Christmas."

"Professor?" Gideon was busily blowing out the candles and secreting the scarab in his amulet bag, all the while mulling over the mummy's recent unanticipated assistance.

"Yes?"

"It's begun to occur to me that, well, George might be a little unhappy at losing any more treasures, if he's still got some."

"Gideon." His father looked at him. "Gideon. Let us try our best to keep fantasy separate from reality, shall we?"

"But you yourself, Fath—"

"Are you joining me? Or would you prefer to stay and keep George company?"

Gideon trotted after his father and Christmas's money.

"Damnable luck!" Emmanuel Wistover groaned as Naseem pulled off his linen shirt and began to examine the bruises growing on his arms. He'd used them to shield his head as he plummeted from the hotel balcony onto the street. That's when he'd let go of the scarab, of course. And now he was one large ache. "Anything broken, do you think?"

Naseem tested the bones of his arms, wrists, and fingers. Finally she shook her head no and pantomimed by letting her own arms go limp.

"Well, I know I've got a few sprains, idiot woman! Any mortal person would! Why I've carted you around all the way from Egypt, putting up with your vapid

41

foolishness, evades me at the moment. And don't just stand there acting as if I've insulted you. Use what little sense there is in your head. Get me a drink!"

Naseem did so, but when she presented the glass, her demeanor suggested she wished it were hemlock instead of whiskey. Wistover didn't notice. He was busy plotting again.

"They must still have it. I'm sure they still have it. I can feel it in my battered bones. And it was magnificent! The largest emerald imaginable, just as the papyrus scroll suggested. And covered with markings! What do you suppose happened to the other piece? Never mind. I must get back into their room again. Better yet, I must follow them, their every movement." He stood, then groaned and settled back onto the bed. "But not tonight. Besides, they would recognize me, even disguised." He gazed up at Naseem, a thought being slowly born in his head. "But they've never seen you, have they?"

Naseem edged away, robes swishing. Wistover's hand shot up to grab at those robes and jolt her back. "You shall be my spy, Naseem."

ᴛʜᴿᴇᴇ

Saturday morning was perfect. Gideon whistled as he left the hotel. He had spending money in his pocket, the sun was shining, and the heat warmed him as it hadn't since he'd last seen Cairo. The only question was where to start the day. Squinting at the sun, Gideon headed into it, east, toward the Mississippi. The French Market made sense. He'd gorge on fat, yeasty beignets and thick chicory coffee. Then he'd wander up the levee and watch the boats. Maybe the *Lulabelle* would be returning. He could escort their panorama back to the hotel and the still-sleeping professor. That would be a pleasant waking surprise for his father. It might even start him off in a decent humor for the day.

There was no hurry. Gideon bypassed the broad,

43

grassy park of Jackson Square to wander at will behind the cathedral and on into a maze of narrow connecting streets, bestowing his smile upon the sweepers, leaping over their piles of carefully gathered horse droppings. Even the flies buzzed pleasantly about his ears.

Behind him, unnoticed, an exotically swathed figure followed, carefully avoiding those same piles.

Gideon slowed down at a corner cockfight, then paused at a bookshop, caught by a novel displayed in the window: *Bleak House*. He wanted it. London might have been a cold and dismal experience, but at least it had introduced him to Charles Dickens. Now he had money to buy the book, too. His first pocket money since New York. Gideon jingled it cheerfully, then pushed through the door to make his purchase.

Later, at the market, Gideon chose an empty table in the sunny, open-air patio of a café and dropped his wrapped book down with a satisfying thunk. His day was improving by the moment—until he looked up to request his breakfast. A surly waiter smirked at him, standing in attendance far too long after the order was placed. Gideon frowned.

"So, it's my money you wish to see, is it?" He flung a few coins onto the table and the waiter nodded and left.

Gideon's fine mood had vanished with the unspoken insult, however, and the arrival of the doughnuts brought no cheer. Here he was, practically thirteen, and even waiters treated him as if he were a babe in cloths instead of the young man-about-town he'd like to be. He morosely bit into one of the pastries, staring right past the plump old Negro woman who was working the tables, selling charms. She, however, noticed the coins still sitting before the boy and sidled up.

"Fine day, young master."

"What?" He swallowed a mouthful. "Oh, I guess so."

"Troubles, son? You got them blues?"

"Could be, if that's what feeling low-down is." He pushed over his plate. "Want a beignet? I'm not hungry anymore."

"Lord, no. They don't 'low me to eat here, they sure don't."

Gideon took a closer look at the woman. "That's silly. You get hungry, too, don't you?"

She laughed. "You truly wants to share them, you come walk a ways with Old Lucy. Maybe I find what ails you. Maybe I gots a cure for it."

Gideon lit up and peered into the basket by her side. "You have something in there that'll make me grow about three feet?"

"Don't know about no three feet. Not 'xactly overnight. But maybe close."

Gideon emptied his coffee cup, shoved his book into his waistband, grabbed the doughnuts, and followed the old woman. They walked up the embankment to the levee together, both eating his beignets.

"You see, I've been this same height it seems like

years now. Look at this shirt." He pointed to the fraying cuffs. "Most boys, they grow out of their shirts before they get a chance to wear them out. Not me. And the professor, my father, he doesn't mind one little bit, because I look more dramatic in his act as a pygmy. A midget! Me!" The words came tumbling out of Gideon. Maybe because he hadn't had anyone to complain to for a long time. Maybe because the frustration had just caught up with him.

"Mighty good beignets, honey. Old Lucy thanks you." She wiped her mouth and adjusted the bright handkerchief knotted around her frizzy gray hair. "Seems to me, what you needs is one of my growth charms."

Gideon stopped. "Well, now. I'm not sure I believe in such things—"

"Not believe! In a charm prayed over by Marie Laveau, the Voodoo Queen herself? Let me look into your eyes, boy."

Gideon obediently raised his face to the old woman's. Her eyes were big, with dark irises, and whites showing a jaundiced yellow. And they were kind. She stared into his own blue ones for what seemed an awfully long time. Then she let out a little humming sound from her throat. Finally she seemed to remember herself and began to speak.

"Anybody believe in charms, it be you, son. I see you connected, connected deep to magic goin' back ages an' ages. Back to Africa. Not my Africa, wet and jungly. Lordy no. Diff'rent Africa. Hot. Dry. Blowin' sand. I

46

see a hand reachin' out to walk with you. Hand be dry as the sands. Leathery as my amulet bags. I see—" But she stopped seeing and let out a little shriek.

Gideon jumped. "Lucy? Ma'am? Are you all right?"

They'd been stopped still in the middle of the bustle of the port, people walking around them with curious glances.

The old woman seemed to come out of her trance. She gave Gideon a harder look. "You don't need no growth medicine, boy. You needs life medicine. Soon. Come through the next few days, worry 'bout growin' up then."

Gnarled fingers worked through her basket, touching first one amulet, then another, as if feeling for their power. The fingers finally halted. An amulet was slowly removed and lowered over Gideon's neck. There the fingers stopped, sensing his other leather thong. Trembling, Old Lucy pulled the scarab bag from Gideon's shirt.

"Hey, don't touch that—"

"Wicked. What you got in there *bad*, son. Get rid of it!"

"I can't!"

He pushed away her fingers, not unkindly, and secreted both amulets beneath his shirt. Old Lucy backed away.

"Don't know if even the Voodoo Queen have 'nuff power 'gainst that one. But don't lose my charm. Don't—" Then she stumbled off into the throng.

"Lucy! Ma'am! Wait! Let me pay you something!"

But the old woman had disappeared. In the crowd, another hovering woman had taken note of the entire interchange. She spun around soundlessly, leaving Gideon, her charge, on the dock.

"The boy has the scarab? He's walking around with a king's ransom in emerald around his neck? And you left him there? Alone in the port of New Orleans? Prey to any sneak thief that comes along? Haven't you learned anything since your father sold you down the river?" Wistover's fist was raised to strike out at Naseem. Then he recollected how sore his arm still was, and dropped it with a groan. "What to do. What to do." He shuffled around the small room, glowering at the cringing Naseem.

Finally he stopped. "It's quite simple, really. We'll merely catch the boy and steal the emerald."

Naseem motioned from the wall she still clung to.

"The mummy? What about the mummy?"

She made the sign for reading a scroll. He remembered. "The other treasure. Of course I wasn't forgetting the rest of the treasure. You think my brain is as small as yours, a mere female's?" Naseem made no reply. Wistover paced another circuit around the room.

"What we need, then, is the boy *and* the mummy. Intact. At least the mummy. And how do we accomplish that?"

Naseem motioned the shape of the boy, then hugged the shape to her body and made running motions with her fingers.

"Take the boy? Abscond with him? Of course. Then we'd have the emerald. Tompkins would trade the mummy for the boy." He stopped. "At least, I think he would."

The professor was staring blearily into the mirror of the washstand when Gideon raced into the bedroom, flinging his lone parcel onto his bed.

"There you are at last." His father held up the straight-edged razor he'd just finished honing against a leather strap. "I think perhaps you'd better do the shaving honors today, Gideon. My hand seems a trifle unsteady. Strange how it's always the finer wines that do that to a man." And the professor collapsed into a nearby chair.

"But—"

"I'm not in the mood for insubordination, young man."

Gideon, still panting, obediently draped a towel around the waiting shoulders, picked up the shaving mug and brush, and began lathering his father's face. He'd had a fair amount of practice at playing the valet since they'd left Egypt. Before that, Rashid, an ancient retainer, had always done the chore, clucking over his father with steaming towels, sharing the gossip of the household in Arabic swift as a plummeting desert hawk. Gideon had always enjoyed watching the daily ritual. In those days, it was one of the rare moments they'd have together, before his father went off to the consulate and Gideon himself sat down with his round of tutors.

Today, however, his own hand was less than steady. His father yelped.

"If you'd rather not shave me, Gideon, you might say as much."

"Sorry, sir." Gideon took a deep breath, trying to still the hands that were acting a lot like Old Lucy's. "But the most peculiar thing just happened to me in the French Market—" The razor slipped a second time.

"Enough!" The professor pulled the towel from his shoulders and wiped the remaining soap from his face. Then he got up to stare peevishly into the mirror again. "Twice! Twice you've cut me!" He held the towel up on either side of his face to stem the flow of blood from the scrapes. Gideon stood back, out of harm's way. His father glared at him from the mirror.

"What is it, then? What is this marvelous event that almost precipitated patricide?"

Slowly Gideon pulled both amulets from their hiding place next to his heart.

"Humbug! Old wives' tales!" Thus had Professor Tompkins responded to his son's recital. Then he'd thought some more, over the steaming hot pot of coffee that Gideon had ordered from the hotel kitchen. Now he sat buttering fresh rolls, staring at George, who'd been returned from the bedroom to his sitting room window.

"Still and all," his father began again, pouring his second cup of coffee. "Still and all, I suppose Wistover could make another try for the scarab. He walked away from his fall last night. And he tends to hold grudges."

"You did win that duel back in Cairo."

"I merely nicked the scoundrel. A flesh wound to the thigh. He didn't seem worth killing at that moment."

"What brought on the duel, anyway, Professor? The servants refused to tell me, and there was no one else I could ask."

His father was staring at George again. "The usual silliness, I suppose. You were too young to understand."

"But there's got to be more to it than that, for one man to challenge another to mortal combat—"

"Not necessarily. Not when it's in vogue. Here, too. Haven't you seen the fencing salons around the French Quarter? All over the place. And that little garden behind St. Louis Cathedral—my saloon acquaintances claim it's the most favored local meeting ground." The professor frowned. "In my instance, it was apparently a breach of courtesy, an impugning of character. I called Wistover an insolent, thieving puppy."

Gideon grinned. "To his face?"

"Of course to his face! He'd just tricked me out of some of my finds at that tomb I was messing about with behind the Valley of the Kings."

"George's? The one in the side of the rock face that you bribed the tomb robbers to take you to?"

"The same. Claimed he'd bribed those Kurna bandits a full day before I did. His mistake was that I came with enough rope to climb down the face of the cliff to the burial cave—while he was off in Luxor trying to buy some!" His father was smirking now, then the expression faded. "But those rascally thieves bilked both of us. All that was left was George and a few scrolls. And neither of those would have remained had they not been covered by a rock fall the crooks were too lazy to excavate. Wistover got his hands on the scrolls when he arrived in the midst of my burrowings for the mummy—"

"But if you were there first, shouldn't everything, including the scrolls, have been rightfully—"

"Truth to say, he did lend a hand when some of the rocks unexpectedly cascaded over my legs, temporarily entombing them."

"Then he wasn't such a villain as all that!"

The professor gave his son a steely glance. "Any man who chooses to negotiate on tomb finds while his competitor is buried to the hip will always remain a villain in my book."

"Oh."

"Anyway, Wistover got the scrolls and we ended up with George. It could have been for the best; I never was as clever at deciphering hieroglyphs as I let on, I'm afraid." The professor sighed.

"So the duel was later, once you'd had time to dwell on ..."

"... the inequities of the arrangement. Indeed."

"I don't suppose the fight had anything to do with your losing your consulate job?" The events of the recent past were finally beginning to make some sense to Gideon.

"Perhaps it was just the final straw. Maybe I had been spending more time in the field than at my desk. And our enlightened consul didn't see eye to eye with me on the subject of dueling, either. He would be one of the few who didn't. Said it was a lot of bunkum when I suggested it was an aesthetic mode of settling difficulties. And I wasn't even the challenger! Was that fair, Gideon? Was that just?"

But Gideon was still busily adding up facts in his head. "You say Wistover got the scrolls from the tomb. Could they, just possibly, have had anything to say about our George?"

The professor's cup paused before his lips. "It wasn't an unknown occurrence. Sort of writing up an obituary about the deceased, pointing out all his fine points to the gods of the other world."

"Then such a thing might also mention the mummy's worldly goods?"

"For example, an emerald scarab, Gideon?"

Father and son looked at each other.

"That insolent, thieving dog didn't just happen to be in either Eulah Landing or New Orleans. He didn't just fortuitously stumble across my advertisement. He's been following us since Cairo!" The cup clattered onto its plate, sloshing coffee in all directions.

"And now he knows where we are. And he's seen the scarab."

"Tell me again about this Old Lucy of yours, son."

It was decided that neither father nor son would leave the hotel without the other's company until they'd made the sale to Claude Christmas on Monday morning. Better yet, perhaps they'd just stay within their rooms for the remainder of the period. It wasn't that long to wait, after all, just a day and a half—at the end of which was the prospect of economic security.

The afternoon was spent pleasantly enough, the professor teaching Gideon some of the finer points of poker. And even supper went well, served in their sitting room by a fawning waiter. It was when night had fully descended that the professor became unbearable. Maybe it had something to do with the full moon. He prowled from one balcony to the other, casting jealous glances at the free citizens milling in the streets below, listening to the musicians, watching ragged acrobats juggle and tumble for pennies in the open square just beyond. Back and forth he paced like a caged lion, until Gideon could stand it no longer.

"For pity's sake, sir, go down to the hotel saloon and talk to someone."

"You don't mind, Gideon? We did agree—"

"I've got the scarab, and I'm not going anywhere, except to bed. As long as you don't leave the hotel, what could happen?"

His father smiled with relief. "Exactly. What could happen? I've got the key to the door. Why don't I just change into something a little less informal. It is Saturday night."

Across the street from the hotel, among the milling crowds, Naseem had been studying the second-floor windows of the professor's suite for hours. She noted the growing frenzy of Tompkins's pacing, noted the silhouette of his figure changing into another coat, knotting another tie. Then there was only the small one's figure, standing next to the mummy near the first balcony, apparently in conversation with it. Naseem nodded to herself and rushed back to the waiting Wistover.

A short time later, Wistover was walking very rapidly through Jackson Square with Naseem to the rear, as was appropriate. "The boy's alone, undoubtedly locked in. He's young, but not stupid. How do we get him out?" He turned his head for the woman's response and nearly exploded. She had fallen behind and was now rooted to a spot several yards back, apparently entranced by a group of beggar performers. Wistover reversed himself and grabbed at her roughly. "Have you gone completely mad? We have no time for this nonsense!"

But Naseem stood her ground, signing until he began to understand. Wistover blanched at her suggestion. "Enter through the balcony? On the shoulders of these dirty tumblers?" She pantomimed again. "Of course. It would look like an act, not illegal entry."

He thought about it. The scheme did have nicely rounded proportions. To return by the same way—the very same balcony—from which he had so ignominiously departed only the previous evening was more than tempting. Yes, it was fitting, even beautiful. Why, he needn't abscond with the brat at all, merely grab the emerald and the mummy and disappear.

Wistover nodded assent at Naseem. He was an adventurer, after all; he could swallow his secret dread of heights for the few seconds it would take to be hoisted onto the second-floor balcony of the hotel. Just as he had overcome the same fear on that cliff face above the tomb. And hadn't that resulted in the mummy's scrolls? His long chase was almost over. Wistover pulled out his wallet and caught the eye of one of the acrobats.

Gideon was tucked into bed, reading by the light of a single candle. In the press of the day's events, he'd entirely forgotten about his morning's purchase. Only with his father's departure had he noticed the book waiting on his bed. It was a relief now to have a little peace and quiet from the professor, to stop worrying about George's very troublesome scarab, to ease into the mists of a murky London fog. He sighed with bliss and turned a page.

At this same moment, Wistover was watching his five well-paid acrobats begin to form a pyramid beneath Tompkins's hotel balcony. Also watching were several score of pedestrians in the midst of their Saturday evening promenade through the quarter. None of them, however, had the lump that Wistover felt forming in his stomach.

Wistover was aware of Naseem standing close behind, silently egging him on. Come to think of it, the woman had been unusually pliant, even supportive, in this phase of his mission. Could she be harboring some thoughts about that emerald herself? Wistover cast a suspicious glance back at her. Was that expectation he perceived? Ridiculous. She hadn't the intelligence to thwart him. No mere servant, no woman had. He returned his attention to the leader of the acrobats, a wiry youth with mischief in his eyes. There shouldn't be any trouble from him, either. It was obvious the young man had been on the wrong side of the law most of his life.

The leader beckoned. Then he jumped lithely upon the shoulders of his three sturdy cohorts spread out in a line, arms extended to catch him. A fifth member of the team leaped up beside the leader, forming the second tier of the pyramid. Already they could look into the balcony, if they chose to turn their heads. An idle street musician, joining in the fun, put a horn to his lips and blew a rousing crescendo of notes.

Wistover stared at the straining figures and gulped. Naseem gave him a hard push. He stumbled forward, and began to climb the ladder of bodies. On the second level of the pyramid, hands hoisted him higher and higher, until Wistover stood tottering, one foot upon the head of each acrobat beneath. The horn blew again, the entire pyramid reversed itself, and Wistover felt himself propelled backward over the wrought iron of the balcony.

Gideon hadn't even noticed the street noises accelerating outside his window, he was so enmeshed in his story. But that trumpet sounding . . . He pulled himself away from the page in time to see a human cannonball shooting into his room. Before he could blink, the form began unfolding itself and was pointing a pistol at him. Gideon grabbed for the bags around his neck.

"Mr. Wistover, I presume?"

"In the flesh." Wistover had managed by now to pull himself upright, not without a few ill-concealed groans. "Just hand over that scarab, like a nice little boy."

"Not on your life."

"My life, indeed!" Wistover snickered. "It's your life we're discussing here." He cocked the pistol and peered around the room. "And where's that mummy of yours? I'll be needing him, too."

Gideon hadn't budged an inch. Maybe, if he could keep Wistover talking, his father would return. Surely it was past time for that. Surely the professor wouldn't keep his usual late hours in the current circumstances. "I wouldn't mess about with George. He's taken a dislike to you."

Wistover sneered. "Let's have no leg pulling. That bundle of bones is mine by rights, and I intend to have him." He jerked the pistol and moved a step closer. "For the moment, though, I'll just take that emerald. Don't bother removing it from the case. I'll relieve you of the entire thing."

Gideon felt beneath his shirt. His fingers touched

Old Lucy's amulet. Perhaps Wistover could be fooled. He began to pull out the leather thong. Just then there was a noise at the door. Gideon's heart soared. His father was back! Unfortunately, Wistover also heard the muffled sounds of a key fumbling in the lock.

"Damnation!" He stuffed the pistol into his pocket, grabbed Gideon by the collar of his nightshirt, and ripped at the leather thong.

"Gideon, my boy. I have returned!"

Gideon felt the thong burst, and in another second Wistover was dashing for the balcony, giving a sickly whistle, and disappearing over the side into outstretched arms. Gideon jumped out of bed to follow, and leaned over the iron railing just in time to hear the crowd cheer. The acrobats were already on the ground, passing a hat. But Gideon's eyes were on the figure of Wistover, weaving through the crowd in victory, a ghostly, shrouded woman at his back.

"*What* has transpired in my absence, Gideon? Why are your coverlets all over the floor?"

Wistover had disappeared into the dark garden behind St. Louis Cathedral. Gideon turned, rubbing at his neck. "We've had another visit from your old friend."

The professor's face paled in the moonlight entering the room. "He didn't get it, did he? The scarab! Tell me he didn't get it!"

Gideon pulled off the original amulet bag and shook out the emerald. "What he got was a bunch of Old Lucy's herbs. And a suitably sized hunk of coal I thought to add to her charm. It seemed appropriate at the time."

His father let out a long breath of relief. "Maybe you did inherit something from me after all, son. Come away from that balcony now. Heavy as the night air is, I think we'll sleep with the windows closed and locked tonight."

Back in his hotel room, Wistover fumbled at the strings of the little leather pouch with shaking fingers as Naseem lit an oil lamp on the table before them. His long nose almost into the bag in anticipation, he let out a huge sneeze. Fine dust flew through the air.

"What the—" He sneezed again. And again.

Impatient, Naseem snatched the bag from his hand and emptied it atop the table. The coal bounced onto the surface, showered by a fine powder of herbs. Naseem rubbed at the dust with a fingertip, then turned to stare accusingly at her master.

Wistover had found his handkerchief, and was using it. He used it a little longer than was necessary, then finally thrust the linen back into a pocket. "Could you have done any better? Tell me! Could you have? It was around his neck, just as you said . . ."

Naseem swept the offending lump and herbs off the table with one hand, causing Wistover another sneezing fit. Finally, eyes red, remaining clumps of hair askew in frustration, he faced her. "All right, then. We need another plan. You are so clever, so blameless. Perhaps you have one lurking in your fertile brain?"

FOUR

Gideon drifted into consciousness on Sunday morning. Something was missing, something necessary to his well-being. He remembered the scarab and clutched at it, then opened his eyes. Sunlight streamed through the windows they'd chosen to leave uncurtained, so they could be alerted more quickly should Wistover try another entry during the night. It came to him finally. Wistover had taken Old Lucy's charm, his life medicine.

That the charm had already helped him once did not escape Gideon. What bothered him now was the nagging feeling that he might need it again—or at least a replacement. Gideon hopped out of bed and did the unthinkable. He attempted to rouse his sleeping father in the next bed.

The professor moaned, turned over, and pulled a pillow over his head. Gideon prodded him a second time and his father sat up with a growl of anger. "No one wakes me unless the hotel is burning down. Is there a fire, Gideon? Is there?"

"Not exactly, sir. But—"

The professor glared maliciously at his son. "This has been discussed in the past. Several times. Even your mother knew better than to wake me beforetimes, Gideon. And I cast more than one servant onto the streets of Cairo for lesser offenses."

"Sir, forgive me. But I have to go to the French Market, to find Old Lucy. I've got to get another charm. And we weren't supposed to go out alone, either of us."

"Harboring superstitions is unseemly and unscientific in this day and age, Gideon. It's 1855. Remember? The era of the steam engine and the telegraph. I'll not have it." The professor burrowed back under his covers.

"You've played on people's superstitions every night we've been onstage for the last year!"

"That's *theater,* Gideon." The voice floated up from under the coverlet with a finality Gideon did not like.

"Father, this is something I have to do. I have a very strong feeling about it. Lucy's charm saved the scarab once, didn't it? If you won't go with me, I'm going by myself!" And Gideon began to dress with determination. Before he'd gotten his boots on, the professor was up, staring at his face in the washstand mirror, looking like the wrath of God.

The café was jammed with late-Sunday-morning pa-
trons, catching up on society and gossip after attending
Mass. The ladies were dressed in their finest, coquett-
ishly batting eyelashes and waving fans. The gentlemen
were equally à la mode, with their frilly shirtfronts and
brass-knobbed canes. The professor swept past them all,
searching for an empty table. Gideon searched for Old
Lucy.

There were several charm vendors around, but Lucy
wasn't among them. In desperation, Gideon finally
tapped one on the arm. She jumped in shock.

"Pardon me, ma'am, but I'm looking for Old Lucy.
Maybe you know her? She sells charms, like you."

The Negro woman was of an age with Lucy, but
taller and bonier. "Don't go touchin' me agin. You got
a bad aura. Felt it comin' when you snuck up on me."
She stopped. "What you want with Lucy?"

"I need her help. She gave me something, but I lost
it."

"Old Lucy give somebody somethin', oughtta have
'nuff sense not to lose it. White boys got no sense,
nohow."

"Ma'am, *please*. I need her badly!"

The woman looked into his eyes as Lucy had done.
She shivered, too. "You ain't lyin', and that's a fact.
Well, then, Lucy be up on the levee this mornin'. Don't
tell her Rosa sent you, though. Don't want no bad blood
on a white boy's account."

"Thank you, ma'am." Gideon had the sense to press a coin into Rosa's hand. She hesitated a moment, then took it.

"Over here, Gideon! I've found us a table."

Gideon walked across the courtyard to where his father was standing. "Later, Professor. I think I know where Old Lucy is."

His father shoved him into an empty seat. "Now. You dragged me out of bed, and I intend to have my breakfast."

Gideon knew from his father's tone that further protest was useless. He'd have to suffer through the meal.

"How could you have allowed me to oversleep, woman? You know we should have been at the hotel hours earlier. Now they've gone out, who knows where!" Wistover stopped to sneeze twice, and Naseem handed him a fresh handkerchief. It had been another bad night. Those damnable herbs in the charm bag had done something to him. "You'd think that out here, in the fresh air of the street, it would stop—*aachooo*!"

Naseem grabbed Wistover's arm and pulled him toward the river.

Several orders of coffee and beignets later, Gideon finally urged his father out of the market and up the bank of the levee, praying all the way that Old Lucy would still be there. He spotted her at the same moment the professor made his own discovery.

"The *Lulabelle,* she's just pulling up to dock!"

"Not now, Professor. There's Old Lucy—"

"Gideon. I grow weary of being led around by you, like a bull by his nose ring. It's not seemly for a grown man."

"It will only take a moment, sir."

"Fine. And settling up with the captain will only take a moment, as well. Meet me aboard ship."

"Father!" But he was gone, into the crowds. Gideon felt a surge of complete nakedness, then shook himself and marched over to Lucy.

"I don't believe it! The boy's right there, in broad daylight. And Tompkins striding off in another direction!" Wistover rubbed at his itching nose and beamed. Naseem's face held a satisfied "I told you so" look, but Wistover ignored it.

"You do have the bottle and cloth, don't you?"

Naseem patted her robes.

"Excellent. We'll just give Tompkins a few more minutes to get out of sight and hearing. Then the boy is ours."

Old Lucy dismissed a customer and twirled around before Gideon could accost her.

"It's gone, and you still be needin' it bad."

"How did you know?"

"Had a dream last night. A mean one. Even went off after Marie Laveau, the Voodoo Queen herself, this mornin'. But I missed her entire. She was off to Mass, then to the Parish Prison to feed the condemned on her gumbo."

Gideon was confused. "The Voodoo Queen? I don't understand—"

"Course you don't. You gots roots right enough, but you ain't yet opened your heart to 'em." All the time she was talking, Old Lucy was fishing in her basket. Now her fingers lighted on another charm bag and she pulled it out. "Did some thinkin' and prayin' myself since that dream. Ain't foolin' around no more. What you need now is my strongest *gris-gris*."

"Gris-gris?"

"We gonna fight back, 'stead of just fendin' off. This here is the most powerful charm I can work." She slipped it around Gideon's head. "You wants your enemy harmed, you gets near to him with this here. You wants him destroyed, you puts a li'l piece of his hair in with it. You got that, young master?"

"Yes, but—"

"You need Old Lucy again, and she ain't hereabouts, you come over to Congo Square and asks for her, or for her man, Zozo. Hear?"

"Yes, ma'am. And let me pay you something this time—"

She pushed his hand away.

"But you must need the money. I don't understand why—"

"I gots a personal feeling about this matter, young

66

master. And you is the only white gentleman ever invite me to dine with him."

Gideon watched Old Lucy walk back into the crowd with her wares, crying, "Powders! Roots! Spells to cure your heartache!" He suddenly felt at least a foot taller. He felt so good, in fact, that just as an arm draped in silks snaked over his shoulder he bolted for the river's edge and the *Lulabelle*.

Naseem's face was a grimace of frustrated fury. She still held the pungent pad of cloth in her outstretched arm, like a cocked gun. Wistover had to force the stiff arm back down to her side. "We'll get him as he leaves the boat. I swear we will, Tompkins or no!"

The professor was just sauntering down the gangplank, followed by a redheaded deckhand balancing their panorama roll over a broad shoulder.

"Ah, there you are, Gideon. No harm done, as you see. We both accomplished our business." He turned around. "If you'll just be kind enough to fetch that to one of those waiting wagons over there, you'll be well rewarded, young man."

"And that'll be the first reward I'll have found on this bloody river, sure enough!"

"Come from Ireland, have you? A fine country, I've been told."

"And seeming finer every day, potatoes and all!"

"Now, now. You must give the New World a chance,

lad. Opportunity beckons at every turn for those with their eyes wide open. Think you can hoist that into the first wagon in line? Mind the two ends, now. That's a precious eight feet of merchandise there."

"Aye, and a heavy one, too."

Gideon watched the Irishman work through the swarm of people, barely missing a few heads in the process. Then he thought he caught something familiar about one of the heads. That hair, sticking up in unsightly clumps ...

"Professor!"

"What is it, Gideon?" His father stopped, and the Irishman, thinking perhaps he ought to stop, too, swung around with his load. For a moment he seemed to have forgotten its great length. A broad swathe was cut through the throng as people ducked for their lives. Wistover, however, had not ducked. There was a resounding thwack, and he toppled, out cold, onto the paving stones.

"Jesus, Mary, and Joseph. Did I do that?"

The professor rushed up and looked down into Wistover's face. Then he grinned at the deckhand and reached for his wallet. "You just earned yourself a night on the town, my good fellow."

Gideon was in the sitting room by the balcony, propped up in a chair next to George. They were both watching twilight fall over the city. The professor had just left for the evening, convinced Wistover was out of action—

at least until after their visit to the jeweler's in the morning. Gideon was clutching at Old Lucy's magic amulet. Surely it couldn't work as fast as it had? He hadn't even known Wistover was nearby on the docks. And he certainly hadn't wished any harm upon him. That is to say, he did wish the man would go away and leave his father and himself alone, but beyond that . . .

"I just don't understand, George." Gideon shifted his gaze to the mummy's face. "I really wish you could talk to me sometimes. You do seem to be on my side, although heaven knows why . . ."

The loose bandages around George's mouth fluttered in the evening breeze.

"Go ahead, smile all you like. But I'd like to tell you about old Lucy and her *gris-gris*. I'd like to know more about the magic business when you were alive. It does strike me that you and Lucy would have quite a bit in common."

The breeze died, and the smile disappeared.

"If that's all you've got to offer the conversation, I might just as well get back to my Dickens. He never seems to run out of words."

The professor rose early, of his own volition, the next morning. He spent some time bathing and shaving. Gideon sat on the edge of his bed waiting, jiggling his legs nervously.

"Do you think you might summon up a little more patience, Gideon?" His father was staring at Gideon's reflection in the mirror. "This is my big moment, after all. I finally get to prove that I can become financially secure on my own."

"To whom?"

"To whom? Why your grandparents, of course. And your mother."

"They're all long dead, Father. Isn't it a little late for that?"

"Never! I can still see Jedediah Brown giving me a flinty-eyed look as he reached into his pocket to hand me that last pittance I had to beg for. Just before we shipped off to Egypt it was. 'Since my daughter is fool enough to cast her lot with you, I'm writing her off. This job and this money are the last you'll ever see from me, Stephen Tompkins.' That's what he said, just like that! And you a mere babe in arms."

"And Mama wilting away and dying before we even reached the Mediterranean."

"Yes." His father frowned at the memory, then shook his head. "Well, wherever they are, I just hope they're watching this little transaction today."

"Do you think maybe they might have been more impressed if you'd really earned it on your own? By working?"

"You don't call this work? You don't call searching for archaeological remains work? And what about the educative value of all those lectures I've given? Doesn't that count for something?"

"Well, if you'd put a little more scholarship into

them, or maybe thought about giving the scarab to a place of higher learning, where it could be enjoyed and studied by everyone—"

"Humbug! Give my finds to the unwashed masses?"

Gideon sighed. "A few miles up the river, we were fairly unwashed ourselves. And if Christmas doesn't really want the emerald—"

"Enough!" The professor slipped into his coat. "Brush down my shoulders, will you, Gideon? I think we shall take a carriage to Canal Street. We'll arrive in suitable style. I have excellent premonitions about today."

Naseem was laying a fresh cold compress on Wistover's head. He was muttering deliriously. "Cold. Cold . . . The emerald . . . sand . . . tomb . . . Too high—can't make it! . . . No, not down! Don't look down! . . ." Wistover sprang upright from the mattress, showering damp cloths in every direction. He grabbed at the woman wildly. "Follow them, Naseem! Follow Tompkins and his whelp! Leave me to my ignominious sickbed. They must be followed!"

FIVE

Devol's was a prosperous jewelry shop situated between a haberdashery and a milliner's on Canal Street. Fashionable ladies, maids in attendance, dallied around the façades, inspecting displays through brightly polished windowpanes. As their carriage hovered outside the door, the professor turned to Gideon.

"Perhaps I'd better take the scarab now. It might appear déclassé having it emerge out of your amulet."

Gideon grunted. His father did like to keep up his little pretensions. Nevertheless, he found the jewel and silently handed it over.

The professor's fingers tightened around it, and his face froze for a moment in an expression akin to prayer. Then he turned the door handle and stepped out of the carriage. "Right, then. This is it, my boy." On the curbstone he fished for his watch and flipped open the case. "Precisely eleven of the morning, as Mr. Christmas requested."

A bell rang melodiously when they entered the jeweler's. Several cases topped with glass were positioned on either side of the room, with plump, velvet-cushioned chairs placed conveniently before each. In one of these chairs lounged Claude Christmas, resplendent in pegged dove-gray trousers and a peacock-blue frock coat. He stretched his long legs comfortably, then ambled over to greet them.

"I like a man who can keep accurate time, even in these southern climates." His hand reached out for the professor's. "Good to see you, Tompkins." Then he nodded at Gideon and thrust out the same paw for him to shake as well. "And you, too, son. How's your mint juleps comin' along?"

Gideon grinned and tried to return some of the manly pressure of the gesture before Christmas turned to business.

"You've brought the bauble? Excellent. Jacques?"

A trim, precise man emerged from behind a curtain at the rear of the shop. "We are ready for the appraisal?"

Christmas nodded at him, then at the professor. "Jacques Devol, proprietor, and best gem man south of the Mason-Dixon line. Stephen Tompkins and son."

Devol acknowledged the introduction, then bustled to the rear of a case and pulled a jeweler's loupe on a ribbon from his pocket. "Gentlemen. If I could inspect the stone in question?"

The professor laid the scarab with ceremony on the countertop, removing his fingers from its touch gently, and at the last instant a little hesitantly. Gideon felt the gesture was in fear for the treasure's well-being now that the moment had truly arrived. With equivalent pomp, Devol settled the red corded ribbon over his head and onto his shoulders as if it were bearing a medal of honor. Next he screwed the magnifying glass into one eye, pulled a lamp close, and picked up the emerald. Gideon and the men crowded the other side of the case, keeping silence for what followed.

It was a show every bit as dramatic as Gideon and the Mummy Professor had been performing upon the stage. Maybe even more professional. Gideon watched in fascination as the jeweler first breathed on the surface of the emerald, steaming it. Next he wiped it reverently with a soft, clean cloth and bore it to his louped eye. The stone was slowly rotated. It was nudged closer to the jeweler's eye, moved farther away, returned again. Gideon found himself holding his breath. It escaped with a hiss when Devol finally looked up, winking the loupe from his eye. Gideon watched the glass plummet to the man's chest, to be caught finally by the ribbon.

"May I have your permission, Mr. Tompkins, to extract the stone from its mounting?" He paused as he noted the look of dismay on the professor's face. "I assure you I will be able to remount it almost immediately, with no damage to either the gold or the stone. Quite often defects are cleverly hidden by such mounts."

The professor nodded a slow assent.

"Very good." Devol opened a concealed drawer in the cabinet and removed a few delicate tools. In a shorter time than Gideon could imagine, the gold base mounting was pried from the emerald, leaving the jewel naked—but still impressive. Devol returned the loupe to his eye and went at the stone again, this time letting out crisp, abbreviated phrases as he shifted it in and out of focus while continuing to revolve it in his hand. "Extraordinary cut . . . Exquisite faceting, with balanced symmetry . . . Pure color . . . No chips or scratches other than the obvious engraving . . ." He looked up. "It appears, in fact, unblemished." Devol paused, carefully replacing the stone on the glass counter. Then he reached into his pocket for a handkerchief and wiped his brow, which Gideon only now noticed was finely beaded with perspiration. That operation completed, he looked across the counter.

"Gentlemen. If this had arrived from any other source . . ." He stopped, apparently to rethink his statement, then repeated it. "If this had come from any other source than gentlemen of obvious quality . . ."

The professor could stand the suspense no longer. "Yes?"

"Well, I should probably conclude that it was merely a green tourmaline—a very fine one, mind you—but nevertheless a stone of modest aspirations."

75

"Make your point, Jacques," drawled Christmas. "I'm feelin' like a thoroughbred just bristlin' for the sound of the race horn."

"And well you might. For I have never seen an emerald so flawless. Or, I might add, one so large." He wiped his brow again, then ran over his palms with the same square of linen. "The stone seems to have total personality: color, perfection, depth, cut, brilliance. We need only check the weight."

Gideon watched as Devol fussed in the hidden drawer once more and brought out a small set of scales. These he carefully set up, tested, and tested again. Finally he set the emerald in one of the tiny pans. Gideon had stopped breathing again. He watched as minuscule weights were placed in the opposing pan, and the scales were at last level with each other.

Devol looked up. The fine sweat had reappeared on his forehead, in a precise band just under the line of his carefully combed, thin gray hair. "The stone weighs in at exactly 102.85 carats."

There was silence.

Devol spoke again, into the hush. "And that is just the emerald itself. Mere weight does not take into account the obvious antiquity of its markings—oddly evocative markings, by a hand the equal of Dürer—or its source . . . Gentlemen, this emerald has all the virtues of a perfect stone: beauty, durability, and rarity."

"So what you figure on its worth, Jacques?"

Devol answered with reverence. "Such jewels cannot

be bought. Either they are won in battle, or they are passed on as an honorable gift." He smiled. "I didn't think that one up, gentlemen, although I wish I had. It was first voiced by a Mogul emperor of the sixteenth century. His name was Humayun, and he said it in reference to the Koh-i-noor diamond. But I suspect the old rascal would have been equally impressed by your pharaonic emerald."

Claude Christmas broke into a deep roar of laughter. Then he slapped the professor on the back. "So where's that leave us, Tompkins? We gotta do a little battle, or you want to talk a human-scale price? Somehow I suspicion y'all aren't of a mind to make me an honorable gift of it." He was still chuckling.

Gideon noticed that his father seemed as bemused as Devol. He shrugged off Christmas's touch and returned his gaze to the scarab. Then his eyes slowly moved up to Devol's. "What's the current rate of exchange for a, shall we say, normal emerald? A reasonable stone?"

Devol had begun resetting the scarab in its golden base. Now he paused in his labors and frowned. "There's no such thing as 'normal' for any gemstone, Mr. Tompkins. A fine-quality stone, however, such as I might carry in my stock . . ." He picked up a tool and meticulously tapped a golden prong home against its side of the emerald. "Perhaps a thousand dollars a carat. No major flaws or imperfections, good color."

The professor thought a long moment, then turned to Christmas. "Taking into consideration everything

Mr. Devol has said about my stone, I would be willing to part with it for double that figure per carat, Christmas."

Christmas's face had become a bland mask. Still, Gideon saw facial muscles almost imperceptibly beginning to twitch around the distinctive scar on his left cheekbone. The man coveted their emerald. Gideon knew it with surety.

"Make that fifteen hundred a carat, and I'll cover old Jacques here's fee."

"Seventeen-fifty," the professor shot back.

"Done!"

Christmas's hand crept toward the stone, now restored to its mount. The professor put a stop to that—covering it first, before pocketing it. "Perhaps we might have a further show of good faith, in addition to the 'holding money' already received?"

Christmas reached for his plump money belt and hauled out another wad of bills. "A thousand do you?"

The professor shook his head no. "Something more like ten percent was what I had in mind."

"A man'd be crazy to carry that kind of walking money around with him in this town, Tompkins. Five percent."

"Agreed."

His belt now flattened, Christmas shook his head. "You drive a hard bargain. But I do, too. See you don't plan any unexpected trips the next few days, hear? Ought to have the rest of the money gathered together by Friday night. Your hotel room."

The professor nodded, the two men shook on it, and

they headed for the door. Gideon was the only one to turn around for a last glance at the jeweler, who looked as if he'd just lost his best friend. "Thank you, Mr. Devol. It was genuinely interesting and educational."

The jeweler gave Gideon a bereft smile. "Never have I handled such a stone. I suspect it's an honor I'll not see repeated in my lifetime."

Gideon and the professor jumped into the first carriage waiting in line for customers just up Canal Street. They never noticed the veiled woman discreetly seated in the closed rig across the street, not even when she trailed them all the way back to the French Quarter and their hotel.

The professor was working the cork of a bottle of chilled champagne in their sitting room. It finally gave with the same sound as those pistol shots that had been flying around just a few evenings earlier. He filled a fluted glass and turned to Gideon.

"Care to join me on this momentous occasion?"

"I'll pass, Professor. One of us should keep a clear head."

His father downed the glass, refilled it, then caught the barbed comment. "And what exactly is that meant to signify?"

"It signifies that I'll feel a lot better come Friday night after we say goodbye to Mr. Christmas. It also signifies that I'd like to see his down payment stashed in the hotel's safe. For that matter, the emerald, too."

"The money, perhaps—at least part of it. The scarab, no. I still feel the same about that as before. I won't have it out of our hands."

"Why not? Our old friend Wistover isn't going to have a headache forever. And for some reason he seems to want George, too. Remember?" Gideon walked over to where George was still propped against his seat, and placed a proprietary arm around his shoulder.

"Hmm. Yes. There is always George and his unfathomed secrets." The professor set the champagne glass on the sideboard and rubbed his hands. "I do believe I could take on our mummy at this moment. How about you, Gideon?"

"No!" It came out harder and more definitive than he'd expected. Gideon tried to justify the emotion that had thrust the word from him. "I mean, we still have our show next week, remember?"

"Poppycock! By the time the curtain is ready to rise we'll be wealthy beyond my fondest dreams. I have no intentions of ever setting foot upon a stage again."

"But you promised as a gentleman—"

"I contracted that engagement as a destitute gentleman. I now consider myself a man of means." The professor reached for the champagne again. "If it makes you feel any better, I can always buy out our contract for a few coins."

"What about the panorama?"

"I'll give them the panorama! Now let's see about our George."

But Gideon stood firm, protecting the mummy. "Sorry, Father. Maybe after next Friday night. For now, I truly believe we should hang on to all of our options."

The professor stopped in mid-stride. "Options. Yes. Perhaps you have a point at that, Gideon. As for now, how would you feel about a few dozen oysters on the half shell? Followed by a lobster, and perhaps a little beef Wellington?" He reached for the bottle and drained it into his glass. "And more champagne, of course."

Gideon realized then that it was going to be a long night. "In that case, maybe I'd better have the scarab. So you can enjoy yourself."

"Thoughtful of you, son, very thoughtful." The professor pulled the emerald from his pocket and surrendered it into Gideon's pouch once more.

Wistover had forced himself from his sickbed. Naseem's description of the jeweler's shop had done it. By now Tompkins was fully aware of the value of that stone. That he hadn't left it with the jeweler Wistover was certain. It was not an object to be relinquished lightly, and the kind of money that would buy it would not be sitting around anyone's shop—even the finest jeweler's in the city of New Orleans.

Now, standing in darkening shadows across from the professor's hotel, Wistover fought off an attack of nausea. To compound matters, a fine drizzle had begun to fall from the sky. He stared up into that same sky and shook his fist. "Couldn't have waited a little longer, could you? Confound you elements conspiring against me, like everyone else!"

Naseem grabbed at his arm this time. She hustled him back into the shelter of their doorway and motioned him to silence.

"What is it, Naseem? I'm near the end of my tether. I'm—"

She pointed at the second-floor rooms across the street. The oil lamps had been blown out.

"They're moving! They're coming out! Prepare the nostrum, woman!"

She shook her head no, and motioned patience. Wistover groaned and sank against the doorjamb.

Gideon had had to pull out the professor's pocket watch to check the time in the closing restaurant. His father was hardly capable of snapping it open, let alone focusing on its hands. Two o'clock in the morning. Gideon stifled a yawn.

"It's time to go, Professor."

"Nonsense. The evening is yet young. Where's the orchestra? I want another tune."

"The orchestra has packed up and gone for the night."

"Don't believe it. Want another tune." He banged at the table. "Waiter! Maître d'hôtel! Bring on the music! Bring on more wine! Bring on . . ."

Gideon caught him as he slumped onto the white linen covering the table. Luckily, the china had long since been removed. There was just the one silver spoon left from dessert, pressing into his father's forehead. Gideon sighed. Would all their nights turn into repetitions of this one? Until the money was spent? Gideon felt for his father's wallet and extracted enough money to cover their bill. He carefully replaced the wallet, then urged his father up. It was not easy. The last hovering waiter rushed over and helped Gideon guide his burden to the door.

Outside, Gideon looked in vain for a conveyance of any kind. None was at hand. And it was raining in earnest now. Could he manage the half-dozen streets from Antoine's back to their hotel? He'd have to. Gideon propped his father up against a wall and took careful aim. He slapped his father, none too lightly, first on one cheek, then the other.

"What is it?" At least his eyes had opened.

"We're going back to the hotel. But you have to help me. I'm practically a pygmy, remember? I can't carry you."

"Absurd. Never were a pygmy. Di'n' start into my own full growth till I turned fifteen. Fine, strong lad you are. Take me home."

"Father! Wake up!"

The professor made an effort. "If you insist." They staggered down the street.

"Now!" Wistover's lone word was choked by Naseem's hand. She motioned silence from their vantage point across the street. He gave her a hard look. "Now or never!" She nodded agreement and reached into the folds of her robes. Then she began to stalk the small one and his unwieldy burden.

Gideon, concentrating fiercely on his job, didn't notice the scuffle of feet behind him until it was too late. When he finally opened his mouth to scream a warning to his father, something soft, with a sickly-sweet perfume, covered his mouth. In a moment he was just a sleepy boy, being carried home by his caring, exotic nanny.

"Gideon?" The professor lurched onto his feet, finally wakened by the cold rain that had run in rivulets over his body as he lay in the gutter. He looked around wildly, remembered, and instantly sobered. All that remained was the echo of footsteps rapidly disappearing around a corner of the gloomy street.

Tompkins's hands gripped each other with passion. He threw back his head and screamed out his anguish. "Bring me back my emerald!"

In the darkness, only one shadow took note of the lament. It didn't respond. Instead, it disappeared into the same black street that the footsteps had.

SIX

Gideon awoke with a groan. Eyes still closed, he touched his head in disbelief. It ached ferociously. What had brought that on? He'd just been walking his father home . . . Suddenly the nightmarish memory came back to him: the footsteps following in the rain, the sweetness of the gag that had covered his mouth. It wasn't really possible, was it? Gideon forced one heavy eyelid open, then the next. Cautiously he tried to raise his head. Bad idea. He twisted it slightly to the right instead.

Something was going on at the other side of the room. He tried to concentrate beyond the throbbing in his temples, tried to make out the shapes. One was a man . . . Wistover. It should have been clear that Wistover would never give up. He was sitting at a little table in front of a lamp. He was holding a glistening shape. Gideon reached for the thongs around his neck. Nothing. Wistover had truly gotten the scarab, then. But what about Old Lucy's *gris-gris*? Wistover would have no need of that, especially if he understood its significance.

Gideon groped around the bedclothes and came up with nothing once more. He inched to the edge of the narrow bed and scanned the floor. The charm was lying there, almost within reach. Should he try for it? Then a voice came, and he closed his eyes again, the better to concentrate.

"At last. The treasure of Tutankhamen's vizier. In my very palm!"

Wistover's voice. Gideon strained to catch an answer, but there seemed none. He opened his eyes again. The other figure, it must be a woman—she was dressed like one, but somehow differently—was waving with her hands.

"Yes, yes, I know." Wistover sounded very impatient. "*One* of the treasures of the vizier of Tutankhamen. And only half of the puzzle. I still need the amber frog within the mummy for the rest of the clues."

An amber frog? So George was still concealing a mystery.

"To think that Tompkins would have sold this for a mere pittance. Together, with both pieces, we—I— shall have directions to the burial place of Tutankhamen himself. Consider the treasures there! One of the last unrobbed tombs of a major pharaoh!"

The woman was gesturing again.

"Don't count my camels? Hah! The mummy is as good as within my hands, Naseem. And its secret." He stopped. "There might even be enough for you. You'd look quite well in the ancient jewelry of a pharaoh's wife."

Something close to a hiss of pleasure escaped the woman's throat.

Gideon shivered. He could feel unadulterated greed exuding from the two figures, surrounding them, almost enveloping him. He had to pull himself together.

"Now for the ransom note. My inkwell!"

It was fetched amid another flurry of graceful hands.

"Don't bring the mummy here? Why not? You think the police might be looking for the boy?"

There was a nod of assent.

"Well, then, where? . . . Some place safer? Some place outside the city, outside the jurisdiction of the local police?" Wistover stopped to think. "Some place where Tompkins would imagine himself to be on equal ground with me. But where I would have the upper hand, of course." Wistover grinned, and his fingers snapped. "A boat. We'll make the exchange on a boat. They've got all sorts of hidden rivers and swamps around here. Bayous, they seem to call them."

He got up and walked over to a window. Wistover ripped the curtain aside, letting in light. "Morning has crept upon us. I think it might be appropriate for me to wander out and purchase a map of the local terrain before I proceed with the note. Do keep an eye on our little prisoner. You may feed him something if necessary, but don't overdo it. I'd prefer to keep him in a weakened state."

Gideon plastered his eyes shut. It would be far healthier if he appeared innocent of having overheard this particular conversation.

Unwillingly, Gideon had drifted off to sleep again. When he awoke the second time, it was from a touch. He opened his eyes. The strange woman was sitting next to him, lightly stroking his fine blond hair. There was something familiar about her, as if he'd seen her before. Yes, somewhere in the past—on the wall paintings of an ancient tomb? He blinked. She noticed the movement and smiled, becoming real in the present. Then she made eating motions and gave him a questioning look.

Gideon struggled to sit up. "Yes, thank you, ma'am. I'd like something to eat." He felt for his head. He was still dizzy, but most of the headache had gone, leaving only an echo of the throb. The woman peered at him anxiously, then patted his face with a damp cloth.

"I'll be all right, ma'am. But what happened to me?"

She drifted up and over to a bureau, returning with a small, brown bottle. He read the label. "Ether? You knocked me out with this?"

Gideon watched the dark woman's airy motions as she pretended dismay. Not knocked out, not hurt, only put to sleep.

It didn't seem possible, but she mimed so well that

he could catch every nuance of her unspoken conversation. He held the bottle out to her and she replaced it on the bureau, returning with a small bowl of lukewarm *café au lait*. She held it to his lips, but he grasped it with both hands and drank without her help. When he'd drained it, she brought a plate of rolls. There was no butter or jam for them, and they were stale enough to be yesterday's, but he was hungry. When he'd flicked the last crusty crumb from his shirt, she was still sitting there, watching him.

"You really can't talk, can you?"

She shook her head.

"Has it always been like that, all your life?"

She cradled a baby in her arms.

"It must be awfully frustrating at times."

Her eyes clouded over, and Gideon thought it was maybe time to change the conversation to something less taxing. "Your name—Naseem, isn't it?" He waited for her nod, remembering too late it was information he shouldn't be privy to. Maybe she wouldn't notice.

"It's quite lovely," he added, her sudden smile telling him he was safe. Relieved, Gideon closed his eyes to bring back his Arabic. It had been so long, and his brain felt so sluggish. He opened his eyes as it came to him. " 'The morning breeze.' Yes, it suits you."

Gideon watched delight dawn on the woman's face. And then he went and spoiled it with his next question. "Are you Wistover's wife?"

Her head shook a vehement no.

Gideon sighed. "Then why do you help him?"

She deftly sketched shackles on her arms and legs. "You're his slave?"

The eyes became misty.

"But he's not here now. And you don't look at all like a Southern slave. You could just walk out the door and leave ..."

She rubbed her fingers together. Money.

"It makes sense." Gideon was putting two and two together. "If Wistover succeeds, you could maybe get some of that cash and strike out for your own life."

She beamed as if he were a genius, then gave him a light, spontaneous hug. Someone finally understood.

And Gideon did. "It does seem awfully hard to get along in this world without money. Seems to be the major problem in our life—my father's and mine—too."

There was a communal look of sympathy before Gideon struggled to get out of bed. She motioned no. "But why?" He might as well play dumb. She went through almost several paragraphs of motions, the end result being what he already knew too well. He was a prisoner, waiting to be exchanged for the mummy.

Gideon shrugged acceptance. "Could I at least have my amulet back?"

Deviousness changed the cast of her eyes.

"No, I guess Wistover's got the emerald, all right. My other one. It's got sentimental attachments."

Naseem bent over and picked up the discarded bag. She studied it for a moment, giving a delicate sneeze after she sniffed at the dried herbs inside. Then it was again in Gideon's hands, and around his neck. He settled back on the pillow. Maybe more rest wouldn't be a bad idea.

After purchasing his map, Wistover strolled to the river to think about a boat. How big would it need to be? And could he handle one by himself? His entire knowledge of floating vehicles comprised the fact that they usually transported him across great stretches of water. Transported him in, generally, first-class comfort, while minions furled sails, or stoked furnaces, or did whatever else was necessary. Maybe larger rather than smaller. There was a lot of water in the Mississippi. Then again, perhaps he ought to hire a boat and crew, at least a captain. Yes. That made a good deal of sense.

Wistover beckoned a carriage for the return to his hotel. He'd best get a note off to Tompkins now, just to lay out the general situation. He could send specific instructions later.

Gideon woke a third time to find Wistover fussing over the ransom letter to his father. Apparently, he'd almost finished it, for there was a long, satisfied silent reading of its contents, and much blotting. Then Wistover was rushing out of the room, informing the woman, Naseem, that he meant to find a messenger boy to deliver it.

~~~

Wistover glanced around the street outside for a likely-looking lad to make his delivery. There were always several hovering around. He beckoned to one, gave him instructions and a small coin, and returned to the hotel. The boy trotted off dutifully, but was intercepted just around the corner by a very impressive man evocatively flipping a shiny new three-dollar gold piece. The boy stopped cold.

"Don't mean to interfere with the carryin' out of your duty, son. Just like to have a little look at the contents, if I might."

The boy grinned and snatched at the gold. "My pleasure, sir."

The big man read the note with amusement and returned it. "I'll be holdin' down this spot when you head on back with an answer. I get a look at that one, there'll be a matching gold piece for you, hear?"

The boy nodded enthusiastically.

"Fact is, I'll be right here the entire rest of the day. Should there be any other messages, there just might be a dixie in it for you."

The boy's eyes widened. "Yes, sir!" He stuffed the message in his pocket, and this time ran down the street.

Tompkins was pacing distraughtly around his sitting room. Nothing heard from Wistover in over twelve hours. Twelve sleepless hours of agony. It had to be Wistover. If he ever got his hands on that scoundrel again, it was highly unlikely the villain would get away with just another flesh wound. Friday evening was rushing forward entirely too quickly. He had to get that scarab back.

As for the boy, well, Gideon could look after himself in most situations. He'd trained him to it. His son could speak three languages, after all. And their time upon the stage had taught him how to comport himself in practically any situation. Hadn't he hauled a fish out of the very Mississippi River? That feat in itself was astounding to a man who'd never dirtied his fingers. Sometimes that boy acted older than he himself. Hadn't Gideon—

A knock shattered Tompkins's thoughts. He rushed to the door.

"What is it?"

"Message, sir."

The door shot open and the professor grabbed for the note. Then he remembered himself and pulled out a coin. "You'd best come in and wait a minute for an answer."

"Certainly, sir!"

The professor ignored the enthusiasm of the response and walked over to the afternoon light streaming from the balcony. Unsteadily, he opened the note, right next to George.

"Mummy? He wants the mummy?"

The messenger boy had been prowling with interest around the fine room. Now his head turned toward the wrapped-up thing with vacant eyes. He let out a little shriek and scampered back to the door.

Oblivious, the professor was staring at George. "And

93

he wants you unscathed, too. Dare I take a chance?" He sighed deeply. "Probably not. Wistover could hardly overlook a few more holes in your chest."

He returned to the note. "A boat? Location and time to be disclosed. The man must be out of his mind. Completely. However . . ." He went to the sideboard for writing materials and swiftly jotted a response. As the messenger dashed off with it, the professor was muttering to himself. "Maybe I should have brought in the police at the start. It's probably too late now."

Gideon was finally slept out. He sat up in bed, fervently wishing for his trousers, which seemed to have disappeared. Wistover was back at the table, mumbling over a large map spread on its surface.

"Look, Naseem. The closest swamp is something called Bayou Barataria. Just down the river here." His finger stabbed at a spot. "That should do it. No point in going too far afield, eh?"

She shrugged her shoulders. The location made little difference to her.

Wistover finally noticed Gideon. "Back with the victors at last, eh?" He fished the scarab out of his pocket and waved it at Gideon. "Take a good look, young Tompkins. You'll not have another."

With a gloating chuckle, Wistover picked up paper and pen and began his second composition. He looked up only once. "Shall we say midnight, Naseem? Yes. That's a sufficiently dramatic hour."

When the messenger boy knocked at his own door, Wistover was ready for him. Visions of a ten-dollar bill floating in his head, the now exhausted messenger rounded the corner of the street yet again. He breathed a sigh of relief. The stranger was still waiting. He held out the letter expectantly. A dixie floated into his hand. The boy stared at it. There'd never been a day like this. Not in the entire expanse of his life. He looked up at the stranger, who was grinning.

"Will there be anything else, sir?"

"Don't get greedy, son. A nasty vice is greed. Just see this last note gets delivered safely."

The boy pushed back his thwarted hopes, then brightened. There'd be a final coin, at least, at the other end. He and the stranger loped off, in different directions, at equal speeds.

Left behind in the shadows, yet another watcher departed, in yet another direction.

SEVEN

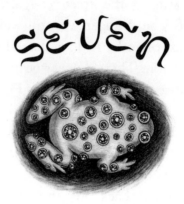

Large clouds that bespoke a coming storm covered the waning moon. Gideon sat in the center of the narrow pirogue, between Wistover and Naseem, with silent oarsmen paddling to the front and rear of them. It was not a very large canoe, as Wistover had bemoaned more than once. Now Gideon could understand the reason for its size as it swept smoothly, noiselessly, beneath branches of cypress trees whose arms dripped Spanish moss. Gideon shivered and ducked as tendrils reached for him. He'd never been in such a dismal, spooky place. He did not belong here.

Night sounds only augmented premonitions of disaster . . . the croaking of frogs, the chanting of locusts and crickets, the beat of drums. Could drums be possible?

Gideon stiffened and listened harder. Yes, there it came again, faintly, but surely, through the jungle of the swamp. *Boom. Boom. Boom-bum-boudoum.* Hollow and threatening. Fear prickled up his spine. Gideon swatted his neck to fight the sensation and brought his hand away wet with stickiness. It was too dark to see a color, but the stain was probably blood. His and the mosquitoes'. Gideon was faintly pleased that Wistover was faring no better, if not worse. He'd been quietly cursing the droning insects ever since their boat had veered from the river. That seemed like hours, even ages ago. How would his father ever find them in this jungle?

Wistover had said it would be easy. They were supposedly making for a landing deep in the Barataria swamp that the local people knew well. Once everyone had made the rendezvous, the exchange could take place, and all could return to their beds. It had sounded simple.

Gideon now suspected that nothing could be simple in such a place as this. He could smell the rot surrounding him, thick and almost palpable. He felt briefly for Old Lucy's *gris-gris,* wondering why it no longer seemed to have any effect on his enemy, Wistover. Unthinking, Gideon let his hand, dislodged from the talisman, drift out—to trail in the black water, to wash away some of the blood. The boatman to his rear hissed a warning, just as one of the many rough logs surrounding them suddenly came to life with a yawning snap. Gideon yelped and hugged his hand to his chest. Alligators! Bigger and more predatory than any Nile crocodile! The boatman's chuckle echoed through the denseness of the night. Gideon trembled uncontrollably, then felt Naseem's hand on his shoulder, a touch of concern, of comfort. He got a grip on his fears.

The professor was rowing in a skiff not that far away. He was rowing because he'd not thought to hire someone to do the work. How far could it be, after all? At least he'd had the sense to procure a guide, who was at the bow of the small craft now, poling and poking, sending directives back to Tompkins. As for the mummy, George reclined to the rear, vacant eyes staring up into the night foliage, his mouth a grimace of scorn where bandages had been loosed by the journey.

The professor unshipped an oar to rest his hand. Already it was blistered as it had never been before. A fine conclusion all this was to his life's work, to the pinnacle of wealth he'd almost attained. He reached for the pistol shoved in his belt, just to make sure it was still there. If Wistover thought he was getting away with this, he had another thought coming. Stephen K. Tompkins would not give up that easily. His fingers felt for the oar once more, then stiffened as curious sounds met his ear. Drumbeats? In the middle of the swamp? In the middle of the night? The sweat on his brow turned icy.

"Jean-Luc. What is that?"

His guide turned, teeth bright in his Creole face. "Man, is the voodoo people. Tonight they celebrate."

"Who are they? What?"

Jean-Luc crossed himself and returned his attention to his pole. *"Malheur.* Bad medicine. We steer clear of voodoo, *monsieur."*

At the appointed place, another skiff lay hidden, pulled carefully out of sight. Its owner lurked under the branches of a vast, ancient live oak, carefully cupping the glowing tip of a cigar in one hand. He was not so stylishly dressed tonight, but what adorned him was appropriate to his mission. A brace of pistols hugged his waist, and a rawhide whip stood in the grip of his other fist. To his rear, preloaded and propped against the massive tree trunk, was his backup assurance: the most accurate gun available, an 1841 U.S. Army model rifle. Satisfied with his armory, he puffed at his cigar, never noticing the dark shapes crouched in the foliage behind him, also watching and waiting. But he did hear the drumbeats, and grinned. His mama would feel right at home out here tonight.

Wistover's pirogue drifted up to the rickety pilings first. Gideon noticed that the man was trembling as he scrambled from the boat, then, in an uncharacteristic gesture of chivalry, leaned back for Naseem.

"You can light the lantern now."

It seemed unnecessary out here in the middle of nowhere, but Wistover was whispering nevertheless. Naseem obeyed, and a little halo of light spread around her silks, sending the swamp beyond even deeper into obscurity.

The boatmen hoisted Gideon atop the landing, where the boy slid on something slimy. By the time he'd righted himself, he had thick splinters in both palms.

"We stay, boss?" asked the leader.

"Yes. No." Wistover dithered before turning to Naseem. She motioned. "That is, pull around the nearest clump over there. Out of sight, but not completely out of hearing. I'll call when we're ready to return."

"Like you say. We wait." The pirogue disappeared silently into the night.

As Wistover began fiddling nervously with his pistol, the sound of oars was heard. At the edges of the lantern light, Gideon just caught Wistover's spreading grin. His captor's figure was almost nightmarish—arms and elbows poking out disjointedly, lengthened by the shadows, with the patchy skin of his face highlighting clusters of hair wildly askew. Wistover seemed to have forgotten for once both his appearance and his inglorious recent history. Anticipation of the moment was all.

"That would be the esteemed professor, come to claim his missing son and heir." Wistover visibly pulled a cloak of superiority around himself. "Not that there'll be much to inherit after the conclusion of our little transaction here tonight."

Gideon tried to ignore the snicker in the voice, straining instead to catch sight of the boat itself. It hove slowly into view, the mummy's wrappings glowing eerily in the night, giving George the appearance of floating, weightless, in the stern of the skiff.

"I trust we've located the correct rendezvous?" It was the professor's stage voice, playing at confidence.

"My compliments. You have. Now, if you'd just raise up the body, you'll have your son's in return."

"Let me see him first."

The snout of the pistol jabbed Gideon's back.

"Oblige me by walking into the light, whelp."

Gideon obliged.

"You seem to be intact." Gideon caught the dryness in his father's voice, felt the eyes play over his inches.

"Yes, sir. But they've gotten the emerald."

"Obviously."

His father's boat scraped the edge of the pilings, and Gideon watched the dark man at the bow quickly secure a rope around the nearest pole. In a moment, George was rising, rising . . .

"Just drop the corpse easy, right there!"

George was flopped onto the scummy landing as all heads jerked in the direction of the new voice. New, but not unknown. Gideon's eyes strained through the dark and were rewarded with the figure of none other than Claude Christmas striding forward, armed as for war.

"Couldn't quite get up the ante for your little bauble, Tompkins. Decided to give a shot at winning the stone in battle." He waved his arsenal menacingly at the figures still tottering upright in the skiff. "Guess y'all better get on up here, too. You might enjoy watchin' the autopsy bein' performed on your mummy friend."

"The emerald, yes," gasped Wistover, all his recent poise vanished as he grasped at Naseem for support, his pistol lifeless in one hand. "But how did you know about the mummy?"

"Ain't nothin' but a little inborn common sense." Christmas talked freely, but still kept a practiced eye on the professor and his guide as they struggled up to the landing. "My mama left me plenty of that. Only not quite enough money. Never does seem to be enough, does there?" He grinned at the gathering endearingly, then got back to business with a nod at George. "Nobody in their right mind hangs on to somethin' that homely without a reason. Figure he's still harborin' a surprise or two." Christmas stopped and beamed upon them. "Which reminds me. First things first." He snapped his whip at Wistover. "How's about I take over that stone now? I'll feel so much more comfortable havin' it in my hands."

Wistover gulped, his Adam's apple suddenly overwhelming his long face. Slowly he pulled away from Naseem to extract the scarab from a pouch around his waist. Gideon almost felt sorry for the man as he held the jewel stretched out in his hand and watched it glimmer briefly in the reflection from the lantern on the dock. He had schemed and plotted and worked awfully hard for it, much harder than the professor had. The brief sparkle was snuffed out as Christmas covered the jewel with his own paw, then quickly tucked it into a pocket.

"There now, I knew you wouldn't leave it layin'

around unattended in your hotel room. The little beauty just seems to cry out for constant companionship, don't it. Like a pretty woman." Christmas was enjoying himself. "Wasn't even that hard, was it?" He patted his pocket. "Guess we'll just move right along to the next event." His eyes were back on George. "Who'd like to do the honors?" Christmas's glance moved past Naseem to Wistover, and ignored the Creole guide to light on the professor. "Nope. Not you, either, Tompkins. But maybe your son . . ." His smile was no longer warm and friendly as it was bestowed upon Gideon. "Com'ere, boy. You seem to take well to directions."

Gideon scanned the group desperately. No one was going to give him succor. Even Naseem's face had closed. He edged up to Christmas.

"See down there by my boots? The handle stickin' out? That's a fine, grade-A bowie knife, son. Sharp as a razor. Pull it out easy now."

Gideon touched the handle. Was it possible? A quick upthrust of the blade might give him the advantage over someone even as large as Christmas—

Christmas's whip flicked lightly over Gideon's back, smarting, and bringing him back to his senses. "Ain't no call for any independent thinkin' here tonight, son. I'll do it all for you."

Gideon carefully pulled out the knife and backed away.

"Good boy. Now you just hunker down there and carve away some of them bandages—" He stopped. "Bring that lantern closer, woman!"

Naseem responded as if mesmerized, and in a moment Gideon had more light on his subject than he wanted. Poor George. Kneeling next to the mummy, he dropped the knife and tenderly smoothed the now ragged wrappings from his face, his neck, his chest. When he got to the hole made by Jed Smithers, the hole responsible for this entire mess, Gideon stopped.

"Doin' just fine, boy. But put on a little speed, hear? Don't mind in particular spendin' the rest of the night in the Barataria myself, but you and the woman might be a little put out by the storm brewin' up."

Gideon lifted his head to listen. Yes, there were now distant rumblings of thunder, and something beyond— or was it closer? Those drums again.

"Pick up that knife and carve!"

Gideon picked up the knife, then stared at George anew. He looked so shrunken, so small and lifeless tonight. George had been his friend, his companion, the only one to bare his troubles to for such a long time. Even if he hadn't exactly been capable of responding ... Gideon raised the knife, then stopped in midair, poised for the cut.

"I can't. I won't!"

Christmas's whip struck again, only this time it wasn't a flicker. Gideon felt the cut it made across his back, like a burning brand, and actually heard a gasp from Naseem.

"Do what I say, boy." There was no longer any feigned camaraderie in Christmas's voice. It was all cold steel. As cold as the blade of his bowie knife. In a blinding flash, Gideon finally understood who his true enemy was.

"George doesn't deserve this. He didn't ask to be pulled from his tomb and dragged halfway across the world—"

The whip struck again, this time with such force that Gideon dropped the knife and was propelled into the mummy, into an embrace that felt almost welcome. He huddled there, arms reaching around his leathery friend, dry sobs heaving his body. Then his fingers felt something sticking from George's back, something that certainly had never been there before. Gideon gasped for air and touched the object tentatively. It was round, hard, with raised bumps. His fingers explored the texture again. The bumps were faceted, like jewels—like the emerald. This was definitely not part of George. The words in Wistover's hotel room came back to him. Could this be the amber frog? The second half of the puzzle? A new gift from the mummy? Gideon's fingers closed over the object as the furies of hell quite suddenly broke loose around him.

Naseem had gone for Christmas first, raging into him like a lioness protecting her cub. Snarling, biting, she evaded a shot from his pistol to rip the offending whip from his grasp and turn it upon its owner, scattering the gun into the swamp. But Christmas was still far from being conquered, far from being turned into a cowering hulk, when—revealed by a flash of lightning—an endless army of figures swinging clubs, spears, and old swords attacked from the surrounding vegetation.

The Creole guide had chosen the moment to flee, jumping into the boat waiting on the bayou, but the professor and Wistover still stood rooted to the landing, ineffectively gaping, their own guns useless without the true will to shoot. Almost meekly, they were led off the landing by the mysterious assailants, into the night. Christmas and Naseem were herded off next, Naseem still clawing at the villain. Gideon, blinking, looked up from George to catch the tail end of the action. Then someone was bending down to him and speaking. That someone had a black face, lined with age and strength.

"Steady on, young master. I be Zozo, come to help."

"Zozo?" Gideon was more than confused. His back was one great smoldering torment, and he was unsure whether his legs could really carry him should he be forced to use them. "Zozo?"

"Old Lucy's man. She seen things, and kept you in her heart. Come now. Somebody else need to be lookin' at you." And the old man effortlessly lifted Gideon bodily into his arms.

"Wait. George—"

"He be looked after, too. Not to worry your fine head."

But Gideon did worry. He craned his neck around Zozo's arms and watched as other dusky hands picked up the mummy as tenderly as himself. Bandages flapping loosely, George joined the procession into the darkness.

EIGHT

Gideon strained in Zozo's strong arms, trying to find respite from his wounded back. Easing against his rescuer's chest, he felt his shirt clinging in bloody strips. He pulled away, tearing skin. A wildfire was raging there, and even the old man's gentle touch cut like knives.

"Easy, young master. Easy. We be there soon."

Gideon swallowed back a groan and focused his attention into the night. The storm was almost atop them, raging with an intensity Gideon had rarely witnessed. There was constant, ear-shattering thunder, and wind now, too, cooling his feverish brow, sending the trees around them into mad dervish dances. And then the bolts of light. Gideon had never seen such lightning before. It shocked him, then opened his eyes to the clearing just beyond.

Centered in it was a long shack, cobbled from wood and palmetto. In the afterlight from a thunderbolt it glowed with a bluish hue.

"Where are we?"

"The meetin' place. The Queen waits upon you."

Gideon's overwrought mind tried to fit bits of information together. A finger touched the charm around his neck. Old Lucy had said something about . . .

"The Voodoo Queen?"

"Marie Laveau herself."

Gideon felt a new tingle of fear. One different from the swamp, and Christmas.

"Don't you fret. She be a good queen. Powerful one. Your friend."

Gideon slumped in Zozo's arms and allowed himself to be carried through the blueness, over a threshold, into the strangest world he'd yet encountered.

The first impression was one of light, towering blazes of light. Gideon blinked and tried to absorb the glare and its surroundings. There were pyres, burning pyres heaped high with logs, and flaming torches set in the walls everywhere along the length and breadth of the huge open room. And other things he could barely register before he was brought before a central throne. It could be nothing else. A huge throne it was, carved from the cypress of the swamps, with peculiar, primitive images bursting out of its grain: heads, snake tails, lizards ... But these faded before the small, ancient woman sitting in splendor upon it, almost swallowed up by it. She was dressed in crimson, and her wrinkled skin was the color of *café au lait*. But it was her eyes that pulled Gideon in: huge, dark orbs almost eating up her face, burning with a greater brilliance than the fires. Gideon broke the contact as he felt Zozo bend his knees and stretch his arms forward, Gideon in them, presented like a sacrificial offering.

"The golden-headed little one, Queen. I brings him careful for you."

Gideon struggled out of Zozo's arms, to stand shakily on his own two feet before this woman. It was appropriate. He should be judged as more than just a child. His legs no longer seemed subject to his brain's instructions, however, and Gideon found himself tottering dangerously off balance. He grabbed for an arm of the throne and his hand closed gratefully over a horned image. On the touch, a keen shock jerked up his arm and through his body, but Gideon refused to let go. He clamped his teeth together and looked up to the woman again.

She neither smiled nor frowned at his gesture. Instead, the eyes pierced Gideon once more and held him suspended. Then a brown hand was pushing damp yellow hair back from his brow, leaving his brain tingling as his body had a moment before.

"It the truth. He be pure of heart, like Sister Lucy say. And he got grit, too. Sand and grit." The fingers moved over his forehead again, pressing a mark upon it. "Keep that heart, chile. It be your protection. And the grit, too. But take precautions, all the same." Rising, she looked past Gideon to Zozo. "He suffer. Set him upon the altar."

The altar? Gideon wrestled with the arms once more enveloping him. What were they planning to do with him? But before he could dwell further on that horrifying thought, he was placed stomach down upon a long table covered with a white cloth. Gideon struggled to look around. It wasn't easy, with the hands now holding him down. Was that something furry standing just before his head? A cat? A curiously still, black cat. A stuffed cat! Gideon's shirt was ripped down his back. He forgot the cat and groaned.

"I believed only we people of color suffered from such cruelties." The queen's voice came to Gideon's ears softly and filled with thoughtfulness. "Don't the white man spare even his own?"

Before Gideon could think to wriggle off the altar, out of the reach of the Voodoo Queen, something moist and cooling was spread upon his back. He sighed and relaxed. The hands were gentle, considerate. The fire in his body went out. So did Gideon for a moment, blacked out into a peaceful, empty dream. It must have lasted only seconds, however, for soon he felt fingers working up his shoulders, down his arms, over his hands, his fist.

"What's this thing the chile protects?"

The patient fingers unclasped Gideon's frozen ones,

singly, until his treasure was gone. George's gift. He'd forgotten. Gideon struggled upright, hugging the tattered remnants of his shirt about his body. He faced directly into the eyes of Marie Laveau again.

"It's mine, ma'am. A present from my mummy."

The queen shifted away to study the object in her hand. She studied it a long time, time during which Gideon took in the hush of the room—hushed even filled as it was with scores of black shapes and fire. And something else. At the edge of the crowd, huddled together on the dirt floor, arms and feet bound, were his father and Wistover. And tied up next to them, Claude Christmas. The first two looked uncomfortable. Christmas was seething. But where was Naseem? What had they done with her? Gideon continued his search and finally located her, unbound and free, standing next to Old Lucy as if she belonged among this strange throng.

"The tam-tams!"

The Voodoo Queen's voice brought Gideon back sharply. What was a tam-tam? In a moment he knew. The drums began their beat again. This time his eyes went through the light to see Zozo straddling a huge, barrel-like drum, striking the tight skin atop it with passion. Old Lucy had moved next to him and now had a fat gourd shaking from her hand in rhythm. The crowd began to undulate to the beat, scores of white-handkerchiefed heads bobbing, white-robed figures swaying, and Naseem in her colored silks standing out in their midst, picking up the rhythm. Marie Laveau swung to the front of the altar, next to Gideon, who was now perched upright upon it. She watched the excitement build in her people. Choosing her moment, she spoke.

"Cry come to us. Cry from long time past. *Aidez-moi!* it shout. Help!"

Boom. Ta-boom boom boom.

"Hear that cry, we do. Won't let us be."

"Houm! Voodoo! Aie!"

"Soul be in pain. We fix."

"Aie Calinda!"

"Bring soul. Bring to altar of your queen!"

Eyes wide, legs swaying over the altar's edge in unconscious acknowledgment of the clangorous music, Gideon watched the queen's followers bring George forth in procession. They stopped just before the altar, holding the mummy in six sets of outstretched arms. Was it possible? Had George been Gideon's true deliverer?

"Houm! Voodoo! Houm!"

"The snakes!"

Eager hands stretched behind Gideon, to a dark statue he hadn't noticed on his other side. From out of the statue came forth snakes; thick, endless, sinuous snakes.

"Houm! Houm! Houm!"

More drums joined in. Calabashes twirled. Dried bones clacked in accompaniment. Gideon was riveted in fascination. The snakes hissed over his head, tongues tasting the heavy air, fangs exposed. Gideon ducked as the serpents missed him and were brought to dance over the body of George.

Marie Laveau was in another world now, weaving crazily around the snakes, George, and his bearers: swaying, bowing, shaking, stamping, foaming at the mouth as in a seizure.

"Soul in pain. Raise him up! Soul in pain. Raise him up!"

She now held a gourd of her own and sprayed the body of the mummy with its contents. Then the calabash was tossed high into the air, and the queen was flinging brightly flaming sparks at the corpse. The drumbeats intensified until they reached a maddening, impossible crescendo. Gideon blinked. Was it possible?

George's linens unwound themselves from his body, swaying in time to the music. The bearers backed away, leaving the naked, mummified corpse levitating in midair, surrounded by a rosy haze. But his wrappings, they were swirling, swirling, separating into a long train, dissolving and coming back together again, changed. Gideon stiffened with tense concentration. It couldn't be.

The bandages were no more. Instead, a finely pleated linen kilt undulated around an unseen body above golden sandals; a foot-wide collar with alternating strips of deep blue lapus lazuli, vivid turquoise, and gold hung where a neck should be; matching wristbands graced arms of air, one unperceivable hand of which held a staff of authority; a robe was draped jauntily across an invisible shoulder. Atop it all was a carved wooden funerary mask overlaid with brightly painted lacquers and gold leaf, and wide eyes alive with polished obsidian.

Gideon gaped. George had indeed been an ancient Egyptian nobleman.

The pace of the dance changed with the wrappings, and the music itself. A flute was heard. It was an eerie flute, high-pitched, with the atonal sounds of the East. As if called from the host by her birth music, Naseem suddenly appeared next to George's glowing raiment. The dance turned into a pantomime, the masked, bodiless costume sparkling with semiprecious jewels working out a story. And Naseem, in a trance, swayed next to the vision, interpreting the story through her vivid miming.

There was obeisance to a greater lord. There was the greater lord's unexpected death. From what? A poisoned goblet of wine? There was great sorrow and a burial procession to a tomb. A hidden tomb. A tomb no human must ever discover on pain of loss of the great lord's—the pharaoh's—very soul. There was the instant death of every member of the burial procession. There was time passing. Much time. Then the discovery of the one mortal who held the key to the pharaoh's secret. A mortal who, though dead, would fight for that secret through eternity.

The music eased away into the night. First the mask, then the lordly garments shriveled before Gideon's eyes. All became a pile of bandages once more. Naseem, almost fainting with fatigue, dissolved back into the watching crowd. Marie Laveau clapped once, and the swarm of living humans in the room jumped.

"You see this story. With your own eyes. The wicked must be punished! Destroyed!"

"Houm! Voodoo!"

"This great soul saved!"

"Aie Calinda!"

In a moment, Gideon saw the amber frog in Marie Laveau's hands. For a long second he caught the glitter of its jewels, the outlines of its hieroglyphic secrets. Her arm raised itself, higher and higher. Then she cast the frog into the nearest burning pyre.

"No!" The cry of anguish came from beyond the crowd, from Wistover. "Not the fire! It will be destroyed forever!" Over the heads of the queen's people, Gideon watched him struggle mightily, impotently, against his bonds. Wistover was ignored.

"Voodoo!" screamed the queen.

"Aie voodoo!" her people shouted back.

The aura around George's body faded, then the mummy itself dropped from its suspension into a pile upon the floor.

Gideon leaned back upon the altar, exhausted. His eyes took in the sudden mad dance of the people, heard the tempo of the drums increasing again; then the room began to fade into darkness in his mind.

It could all be a delusion, a hallucination. It had to be. Everything. Everything since walking his father home from the restaurant last night. Ether must be a strange drug, after all. That was the only explanation. Now he just wanted, just needed quiet. But those drums. They kept beating insistently. They wouldn't let him be. Gideon forced his eyes open again.

Marie Laveau and her people were still dancing. All of them were dancing, unconscious of anything else. Around and around George's body. Even Zozo and Old Lucy and the other musicians. Where, then, was the music still coming from? Gideon searched for an answer and found only his father's form, back in the shadows, still bound. A thought wakened in Gideon's brain. Slowly, very slowly, he edged to a corner of the altar. Cautiously he slipped off the side. Carefully he wove his way through the undulating bodies, pausing only to grasp on to Naseem and lead her docilely away. Gideon stopped in front of his father and the others. It was Christmas who spoke first.

"The knife, boy! Quick! In my other boot! Can't get at it trussed up like this."

Gideon was not in his brightest form, but gradually he managed to find the other knife, stopping every few seconds to glance back at the orgy of dancing behind him and to Naseem, still entranced, near his side. Once it was in his hand, he gazed at the tool a long moment, as if deciding on its use.

"Cut the ropes, Gideon!" It was the professor.

Gideon straightened up. Time seemed to have lost its meaning. Again without haste, he began his task. First his father was freed.

"Get on with it!" That was Wistover. Gideon looked at his father.

"The emerald. Get it from Christmas."

Gideon placed the blade of the knife between his teeth and felt Christmas's pockets. The man was stiff with suppressed rage. Gideon found the emerald and carefully added it to Old Lucy's *gris-gris*. Then, quite deliberately, he took the blade from his teeth and sliced a single one of Christmas's long hairs from his head.

"What you doin', boy?" It came out of clenched teeth, in a snarl.

"Just collecting precautions, sir." Gideon stuffed the hair into the *gris-gris* and tightened the strings of the amulet around his neck. He looked to his father, who was nervously rubbing his wrists. "What shall I do with these two, Professor?"

"Leave them to be sacrificed! What do I care?"

"I'm not sure that would be Christian, Father. Under the circumstances."

Wistover was biting his lip, drawing blood, trying to contain himself. Finally he could stand it no longer. "In the name of heaven! Undo me, boy! I swear this business is finished. Forever!"

Gideon didn't bother to glance at his father again. He methodically sawed through Wistover's bonds, leaving only a last strand connected to both arms and feet. Then he gave Christmas a look of appraisal. Christmas was struggling hard within himself, too. The words finally blurted out.

"On my mama's grave, I swear the same."

Gideon considered. Christmas seemed to think a whole lot of his mother. He wished he'd had the chance to find the same feelings about his own. But still . . .

"No! Are you crazy, Gideon?" His father was reaching for the knife. "After what he almost did to us?"

"I swear! Listen to me, boy! You leave me here, they're gonna murder me!"

Gideon pulled away from his father, glanced back at the dancers, then saw the sweat of fear on Christmas's face. Even a man who'd done what he had deserved another chance. Gideon undid his foot ropes, leaving Christmas's arms bound behind his back. Now his job was almost finished, except for one thing. He looked around the room. "What about George? I don't want to leave him."

The professor was shaking his head over his son's folly. "George is, I suspect, in his element. For God's sake, let us flee!"

Gideon stood undecided a moment longer, then snapped the final threads of Wistover's bonds before his father was dragging him out the door. They were off again into the night, Naseem trailing slowly behind. The sounds of revelry were drowned out by the pouring rains that now deluged them.

"Which way to the boats? The landing?"

No one knew. No one cared. All fled from the clearing, still eerily aglow in blue.

NINE

They could have fled in opposite directions, but some perverse instinct had kept them—all the old adversaries—together, like a pack of crazed dogs, or maybe hungry wolves. Gideon didn't want to think it was the emerald. After all, there'd been vows made, and sacred promises.

Now they'd been thrashing through the flooded undergrowth for too long, following the professor's frenzied lead. Were they flailing about in circles? Gideon tried to listen for the sound of rain falling on deeper water, tried to regain some sense of direction, but could not concentrate, could not do more than mechanically make his feet move. Drenched to the very bone as he was, the Voodoo Queen's ceremony was still flashing through his head. Not all the rain in the heavens could wash it from his mind.

"George's dance. He was amazing." Gideon hadn't realized he'd uttered the thought aloud until his father stopped his forward plunge just ahead.

"What?" He barked out the question raggedly as Wistover bumped into Gideon from behind.

"I was thinking about George. What the queen did to him. He looked just like one of the gods on the wall paintings in the Valley of the Kings."

"Are you delirious? What are you going on about? We're trying to save our lives, find a way out of this cursed jungle. Remember? Move, Gideon!"

Gideon did not move. Instead, he stolidly wrung water from what remained of his shirt. The gashes across his back were beginning to sting again, so he knew this piece of the nightmare, at least, was real. "I was talking about George, Professor. Coming alive as he did. At least his wrappings."

Wistover let out a short laugh. It would perhaps have been longer, but he was out of breath, too. "Your son and heir appears to be a case for the madhouse, Tompkins. Bestir yourself, boy." Wistover prodded at Gideon, who was blocking what might possibly have been a path. "My boatmen won't wait forever."

Gideon stood rooted to his spot of jungle, more water cascading down his face as he stared at Wistover. "Did you see nothing?"

"We saw a lot of ceremonial nonsense around the mummy, then that crazy slave dance."

Gideon pushed past Wistover to Naseem at his rear. "And you, Naseem? You who told George's story. Do you remember nothing, too?"

The rain suddenly slackened, and the slowing winds pushed a mass of clouds from one edge of the moon. A single beam of light caught Naseem's face. She nodded at Gideon and swayed for a moment in the rhythm of George's dance. Naseem knew. She had seen. Gideon suddenly smiled. Someone else understood what he had experienced.

Claude Christmas huffed up to the gathering, and the light moved for a moment across his face, too. His old scars were joined by dozens of new ones. They were tiny bloody lashes made by tree limbs his bound hands could not save him from.

"Out of my way. I've had enough of the Barataria for one night!"

"And did you see George dance, Mr. Christmas?"

"That dried-up mummy? You're rounding the bend, boy. But before you do"—his voice softened, turning into a plea—"how's about freein' up my arms here? You've still got my last knife. Our only weapon."

"No insult intended, sir, but you must really believe me insane!"

"Hey, I didn't mean to really hurt you, boy. A few little scars—made a man out of you is all."

"Indeed. And I intend to think like one in future." His head suddenly cleared, Gideon spun about, chose a new direction, and set off.

~~~

They must be nearing the water channel. The spongy ground now sank Gideon nearly to his knees at each step. And something new had been added. It looked like grass, but had grown to wild heights and cut like a saw when it was touched. Gideon backed away from it and waited for his father to catch up.

"Where are the others?"

"Behind," the professor gasped. The storm had now passed completely, and the moon's light showed that his father had not escaped from the jungle's touch, either. His coat was in shreds, and his face welted. Gideon looked up at the moon. Had it not yet begun its descent? Would this night never end?

Gideon forced his thoughts back down to the swamp. "What about Christmas? I haven't heard him for too long."

"What mischief can he get into, bound as he is?"

Gideon shook his head. He didn't want to voice the answer to that. Instead, he squelched on, rounded a clump of the wicked grass, then a group of cypress, and almost toppled into the bayou itself.

"We found it!" he yelled in relief. "And there's a light just downstream. Could it be the lantern, where it was left on the landing?"

His father shoved ahead, his longer legs making the distance quickly. "It is the landing! We're saved!"

Gideon pawed through what remained of the sopping jungle between himself and the landing. He was no longer squeamish about frogs and snakes and other slimy things. Even the Spanish moss that drifted around his shoulders and into his eyes no longer gave him the shakes. As for the mosquitoes ... well, they'd already made such a banquet of him, there was little left to be offered up. He didn't even consider scratching. Once begun, it would be an endless job. Gideon panted through the last of the morass and finally was hauling himself onto the moss-streaked boards of the landing. There he lowered himself, put his head into his hands, and tried to take stock.

He could let himself go. It would really feel good. Gideon couldn't remember the last time he'd cried—outright, aloud—but somehow it felt as if it would help, right here and now. He'd kept himself together for so long. He wanted to get out of this jungle. He wanted civilization, with civilized people. Why couldn't somebody else take over for a while? Why was his father so useless? Why hadn't Wistover brought his map of the bayous so they could find their way back? Why wouldn't any of the adults take any responsibility? He looked up. Where exactly was he? And where was he going from here?

The darkness was still deep. And a late-night silence had set in. Neither gave him any answers. Now there was just the sound of his father, breaking into that silence, calling madly for the boatmen.

"Ahoy! Jean-Luc! Anyone!"

The only response was more silence.

The professor turned from the edge of the landing. "He's gone. Deserted me!"

"Do you blame him?"

"I knew I shouldn't have paid him in advance!"

"It doesn't matter. He would've been gone anyway. Any sane man would've been gone."

"Hired help just cannot be trusted anymore!"

"Grow up, Father. This was self-preservation pure and simple."

"And what of our preservation? How shall we escape this accursed jungle?"

"We could always hunt for the voodoo people again. Old Lucy was there. I'm sure in the light of morning—"

"No! Never!"

Just then Wistover groaned onto the landing, Naseem giving him a helpful shove up. This time he did not turn around to offer her a chivalrous hand. Gideon forced himself to his feet and did the honors instead. She gave him a grateful nod. Her silks had seen better days, but her bearing was still stately. Good, Gideon thought. He turned to Wistover.

The man was a wreck. He had scratched where Gideon hadn't. Now, in the pool of lantern light, Wistover was a mass of inflamed bumps, looking like a smallpox victim in his last gasp. He'd lost his jacket, and there were some curious flat, sluggish creatures adhering to his bare arms and neck. Leeches?

Wistover ignored everyone and everything as he strode with a last burst of purposefulness to the edge of the landing to bellow out his own calls for help. Only when it became obvious that his boatmen had also decamped did he turn back, in total defeat.

"Stranded! Stranded at the bloody end of the world! With nothing to show for my efforts. There can't be anything worse than this!" He raised his head to the heavens and howled out, "I challenge you to prove there's nothing worse than this!"

No, Gideon prayed. No. Don't beg for more.

But he was too late. Footsteps crept up behind them. Then they didn't creep anymore, but became distinctive, assured.

"My mama always said to watch what it was you prayed for. Could be it might all come true."

Gideon spun around. Morning must be coming at last, for Claude Christmas stood out in perfect definition. And so did his powerful rifle.

"Your hands," gasped Wistover.

"Always knew there was some purpose to saw grass. Figured it out tonight." Christmas waved a bloodied, lacerated wrist at them, then firmly grasped his weapon once more. "Too bad about that little doodad we lost to the voodoo people, but I figure if I end up with what I came for, can't count the night a total loss." He grinned. "Can I?"

Gideon gulped. Christmas was the one who was insane. He'd figured out the enemy part, but hadn't caught on to the madness: that leer . . . the pitiless gleam in his eye . . . Now it was too late.

"Tell you what I'm gonna do." Christmas toyed with the gun. "Just so y'all understand how much I really want that emerald, I'm gonna start off with the woman first." The barrel turned to Naseem. "Know I only got one shot, but I'm real quick at reloadin' this here muzzle." He smiled at Gideon. "You kinda like her, don't you, boy? Don't take too long to think about it, now."

"But your sacred oath, on your mother's grave. Your honor!"

Christmas howled. "Thought I told you long time past 'bout New Orleans honor, son. And what is honor? A word. What is in that word 'honor'? Air." He calmed down to a chuckle. "My mama, bless her, be rollin' in her grave with glee just about now, waitin' for the proper denouement to this little play piece." Christmas sobered and tightened his bead on Naseem. "You got ten seconds to toss me that *gris-gris*, emerald an' all. Nine seconds. Eight . . ."

Gideon tore off the charm and flung it at Christmas's feet before he'd reached four.

"Good boy. Didn't take no thought at all, did it?" Christmas stooped to pick up the thong and wrap it around his bloody wrist. "Now I'm gonna fade out of here easy. Only I don't want to be followed, hear? Just to make sure, I'm gonna do a little hobblin' with this ol' gun. Give y'all somethin' to busy yourselves with in my absence." He began to raise the rifle again, and Gideon suddenly knew what Christmas meant by hobbling. One of them would be wounded, if not worse.

Gideon was the closest, so it was he who sprang. To his surprise, he wasn't alone. As Gideon's small body crashed into Christmas's, he heard movement from behind. Just then the gun went off. Its recoil bounced Gideon back onto the landing. He glanced around quickly. Had the shot caught anyone?

Maybe not. His father and Wistover were now atop Christmas, wrestling the rifle from his hands. Just in the background, Naseem was pulling at it, too. She had hidden strength, and the weapon came loose in her grip. Gideon watched her hold its weight in her hands for a split second before she turned to heave it into the river. The three men were still wrestling, oblivious. Gideon could tell it wasn't a fair match, even two against one. Christmas's power was prodigious. Or maybe it was the madness that made it so. Gideon watched his father fall out of the heap first, to sprawl backward onto the landing, stunned. But Wistover fought on, biting, scratching, trying always for the amulet wrapped around Christmas's wrist. The two combatants rolled closer and closer to the edge of the landing, closer to the edge overhanging the bayou. Suddenly Wistover uttered a loud cry and let loose.

"My eye! He's gouged my eye!"

Then Christmas was on his feet facing the defeated, teetering on the very edge of the brink. Giving a shout of triumph, he held out the charm. "I still got it, Mama! I won it in battle!"

Gideon watched the crazed conqueror swing the thong once more in victory. Before his eyes, the bag slipped from Christmas's grasp, made an endless arc across the sky, and fell, clear into the bayou itself. Or did it? There was no splash, but there was a sharp snap and grinding of teeth. Christmas spun around, unbelieving.

"Gators. Gators got my stone. Ain't no gator gonna do Claude Christmas like that!"

Horrified, Gideon watched as Christmas calmly stepped off the edge of the landing. He forced himself to crawl to the same spot. Gripping the rotting wood, he peered over the edge.

Christmas was thigh-deep in the murky waters, wrestling with a ten-foot alligator. Now he was on its back, trying to force open the long jaws. It looked as if he might succeed, until the creature gave a practiced flip of its tail and flung Christmas into the water again. Christmas came up spitting and cursing and met the gator head on. For a moment, Gideon almost believed it might be an even match, Christmas's superhuman strength ripping at the gator's neck, the gator hissing and snorting in rage, seeking access for its jaws to open. Finally, by dint of brute, powerful poundage, the monster forced its mouth agape. Rows of shiny, razor-sharp teeth glinted, then snapped shut on Christmas's arm. His howl of anguish and frenzied splashings brought other monsters gliding into the fray. Gideon tried to avert his head from the sight, but couldn't. The waters roiled as in a storm, nothing but a mass of snapping, biting, snarling jaws. Then there were a few satisfied burps, a briefly floating boot, and silence. Gideon turned away and struggled to his feet.

Wistover had his good eye uncovered. He had seen what happened. "The last half of the puzzle! Gone forever! Tutankhamen's tomb lost for eternity!"

Naseem passed the prostrate professor and her master, who was now falling into mumbling incoherency. She stopped next to Gideon. Slowly she put an arm around his shoulder. Then she raised his face to the east. He looked.

"The sun. It's rising, Naseem."

TEN

Gideon found Christmas's skiff hidden amid thick roots and overhanging vines not far from the landing. He was settling the numbed survivors into it when a low hum rent the air. Even Wistover bestirred himself to peer through the foliage with his one good eye.

"What next?" was all he uttered. It was sufficient, succinctly phrasing the thoughts of them all.

Gideon left the still-grounded boat to find a better vantage point. Behind a cypress, he waited while the hum expanded in the soft dawn air. Slowly the hum became a chant:

L'Appé vinie, li Grand Zombi,
L'Appé vinie, pou' pour pays!

The patois smoothly translated itself into Gideon's mind. "He is coming, the Great Zombi. He is coming, to make for home!" Gideon sucked in his breath and watched.

A slowly straggling procession worked its way onto the landing. There were the dancers from last night's ritual, their robes no longer crisply white. There was Zozo, carrying a smaller drum. *Boudoum. Boudoum.* There was Marie Laveau, the Voodoo Queen, now only a harmless old woman, but still carrying herself proudly. And behind her came a small pirogue, held by a half-dozen followers. Lying in splendor within the pirogue was George.

They were all on the long landing now. The pirogue was held steady as the chanters filed past the mummy a final time in respect. When Marie Laveau made a sign, the pirogue was gently eased into the bayou.

"Li Grand Zombi, li Grand Zombi!"

Gideon watched as the boat, masterless, bobbed uncertainly for a few seconds. Then, as if certain of its own mind, it caught a current and headed unerringly toward the Mississippi, the delta, and the sea.

Gideon felt a stinging in his eyes and wiped away an unexpected, belated tear. *"Bon voyage,* George. I hope you make it," he whispered.

Unnoticed, Naseem had appeared at Gideon's side. Her eyes were tearless, but she was watching the mummy's escape to freedom with unbridled envy.

When Gideon turned to the landing again, the voodoo people had disappeared, merged back into the jungle.

They'd been rowing for some time now. At least, Gideon and Naseem had, taking turns. Gideon had kept a watchful eye for George's pirogue, thinking maybe to give it a helpful shove in the right direction, should it be found grounded. But though they'd followed the same current, the mummy had vanished completely.

Gideon had aided Naseem in binding up Wistover's injured eye with her headcloth just before they'd embarked. The woman looked different now, without her shrouding, as if she could face the world out of the shadows, head on.

As for the professor, well, he was just beginning to peer out from what seemed to be an aching head.

"Where are we, Gideon?"

"Trying to make our way back to the Mississippi, Professor."

"And thence?"

"I couldn't say. But, without George, you've finally got an honorable reason to break our last stage engagement."

"Don't mention the word 'honor' in my hearing, boy. Ever again."

"No, sir."

Wistover stirred in the bow. "You're right for once, Stephen. Damned lot of nonsense, that honor business. To think it even precipitated a duel between us in a former life. Bah!"

The professor creaked his body straighter in the stern. "Has it ever occurred to you, Emmanuel, that none of this would have happened had we amicably settled our earlier grievances?"

"You mean shared the booty in the mummy's tomb together, instead of fighting over it?"

"Indeed."

Wistover scratched absently at his inflamed face. "You might have a point, Stephen. Unfortunately, as with most things, wisdom sometimes comes too late."

The professor cleared his throat. "You didn't, by any chance, think to take a rubbing of the scarab's etchings, did you, Emmanuel? When it was briefly within your possession? That cartouche on its back, for instance?"

Wistover scratched some more, while Gideon relieved Naseem at the oars. "As a matter of record . . . Yes, I did manage that little thing."

"Would that rubbing be on your person?"

"Well . . ." Wistover hesitated, then gave in. "In point of fact, it's sitting safely back in my hotel room."

Gideon couldn't believe this conversation was taking place—not after the events of the recent past. He glanced back at his father, who seemed deep in thought, then shoved into another oar stroke. They'd gotten through the worst of the swamps now, and the sun was beating full and heavily onto his bare, lacerated back. It almost felt good. Gideon accidentally flicked some spray onto his father, breaking his silence.

"Really, Gideon! You could have some concern for the sufferers among us!"

133

The comment wasn't worth answering, so Gideon didn't.

"I said it was safely back in my hotel room, Stephen."

"Yes, of course. And might it have the beginnings, the mere inklings, of an appropriate direction in which to search for the tomb?"

"It might."

The professor sighed. "If you don't mind a personal question, Emmanuel, how are your finances fixed at the current time?"

"Badly. To put it more bluntly, they are nearly nonexistent. If you hadn't led me on this wild-goose chase—"

"I never asked you to follow us, Emmanuel. Never!"

Wistover was scratching again. "Granted. How are you fixed?"

Gideon glanced anxiously back at his father. He wouldn't give away their little nest egg, would he? That money from Christmas had to be legally theirs now, and morally, too, with Christmas and the alligators the current owners of George's emerald. Gideon needn't have worried. His father's face had taken on a secretive look.

"Not well, either. Not well at all. However, there just might be enough to get me—or possibly us—back to Egypt."

"As partners?"

Gideon groaned.

"Why not. As partners."

Around the next clump of cypress the Mississippi sat, waiting.

"You do have the tickets, don't you, Gideon?"

They were standing on the levee of the port of New Orleans a week later, Gideon and his father, Wistover and Naseem. Their baggage stood at hand, and the first call for boarding the ship to Europe had just been made. Gideon felt inside a jacket pocket and pulled out a ticket. "Yes, sir. Here it is."

"It? Where is yours? You promised to take care of these little details during my convalescence, Gideon. I trust I have not overestimated your competence?"

"No, sir, I don't think you have."

"Come, come, boy. The purser waits by the gangplank."

Gideon took a deep breath and squared his shoulders. It was now or never.

"I'm not going with you, Professor."

His father's hand had already reached for one of the shiny new valises. "You're not ... What?"

Gideon smiled. It was getting easier. "I'm not going with you. I have no desire to upset any more mummies. I thought I might give my birthplace a second chance— off the stage."

The professor was now staring at his son as if he'd finally and truly taken leave of his senses. Wistover, nearby, two tickets sprouting from his own hand, had caught the gist of the conversation. "Having a little family dissension, Tompkins?"

Wistover was waved off. "Entirely my business,

thank you." He bore down on Gideon again. "Exactly what do you expect to do here, then?"

"I thought I might finish my schooling. After that—"

His father did not wait for the afters. "And what do you propose to use for money, may I ask?"

Gideon shrugged. "I've cashed in my ticket, for one thing. For another, I took my share of Christmas's money."

"Your share!" His father's face had gone pale and threatening. He took a step closer.

"Don't bother searching for it, Father. It's not on my person."

Naseem was now intervening, coming between father and son. She took Gideon by the shoulders, and gazed into his eyes, begging. Then she let go and motioned.

"You want to come along with me?"

Naseem nodded a vigorous yes. Wistover caught that and barged over. "Just one moment, here—"

Naseem elbowed Wistover out of the way, keeping her glance steady on Gideon.

Gideon rethought the situation quickly, his brow furrowed. It would be someone else to be responsible for. He knew he could do it, but . . . "All right. I could take care of you, Naseem."

No! Her gesture was emphatic. Her hands locked together, making a symbol of equality and strength. We will take care of each other.

Gideon smiled as the ship's horn sounded. "Yes, I'd like that."

"Last call to board the *Sea Star,* bound for Liverpool! Last call!"

Naseem turned to Wistover and plucked a ticket from his hand.

"But you can't do that!"

"Yes, she can. We both can." Gideon shoved a forgotten valise at his father. "I'll send word to the consulate in Cairo when I settle in. Just in case you might be interested." Then he bent down for his own satchel. As his fingers grasped the handle, Gideon caught sight of his frayed shirt cuffs stretched above his wrists. He grinned. Even without Old Lucy's charm, he seemed to be growing at last.